Kent Dellaire

Frederic, The King of Arden

EPICUS Publishing Company

Frederic, The King Of Arden
Written by Kent Dellaire

Visit Website: kentdellaire.com

Cover Design: Bruce E. Speed
speedco@mail.com

First Edition
ISBN-13: 978-0-9816132-1-5

* *

Other Books Written
By
Kent Dellaire:

Billy The Kid, An American Epic Poem
ISBN-13: 978-0-9816132-0-8

PREFACE

V

Frederic, The King Of Arden, is my second epic poem. Like my first epic poem, Billy The Kid, An American Epic Poem, I have justified a page, naturally. By that I mean using a word with the exact length needed to complete a line of verse, so that all of the verses line up evenly on the right side of the page (except for the punctuation). I like to think of this as a kind of mosaic, where different size words fit into place to make an image, in this case a word picture. I doubt if this could be done without computers, since they allow for fast editing. To me, the benefit of this outweighs the difficulty, since close rhythmic patterns are developed, which help to further the drama of the story.

Since our modern world has only rare examples of epic poems, I have looked to the Renaissance for inspiration, hoping to give rebirth to this once noble art form. Therefore, it will be up to the reader to judge, as to how far I have succeeded or failed. In my first epic poem, I rhymed every other line, and used very little punctuation, so as not to disrupt the flow of the poem. However, in my second epic poem, I used blank unrhymed verse and traditional punctuation, having altered this method only on occasion. In addition, each page is given a title, and tells an episode within the story, which I further divided into four books, since the story seemed to have natural breaks there.

Originality is always hard to achieve. But I have done so in justifying a page, naturally, and by reinventing ancient symbols, so that they apply to the modern world. The Sword of Tarsus, the Tree of Life, and the black Dragon are examples of these. In addition to this, I believe I am the only author to have used Near Death Experiences in an epic poem. Several characters relive these "experiences" again, as it were, in the context of the story. I hope everyone who reads this book will see the importance of these real testimonies, and what they may mean for the rest of us. If asked what are my epic poems about, I would have to reply that they are always about the same thing, good verses evil, the eternal struggle between these two forces, and their tragic or benign results. I sincerely hope that you will enjoy reading this epic poem.

Kent Dellaire

CONTENTS
VI

BOOK NUMBER ONE

———————————

CONTENTS
VII

CONTENTS
VIII

BOOK NUMBER TWO

CONTENTS
IX

CONTENTS
X

BOOK NUMBER THREE

CONTENTS
XI

BOOK NUMBER FOUR

CONTENTS
XII

CONTENTS
XIII

CAST OF CHARACTERS

Frederic - The King Of Arden
Edmund - Younger Brother To The King
Gertrude - The Queen Mother
Harold - The Deceased King Of Arden
Kathleen - Wife Of King Frederic
Malcolm - Knight Errant, First Husband To Kathleen
Jasmine - Kathleen's Daughter By Malcolm

Lord Dune - Baron To King Frederic
Dame Rachael - Wife Of Lord Dune
Chester Dune - Son Of The Dunes
General Killarney - General Of The Ardenians

King Hooligan - King Of Pazmania
Prince Paragon - Son Of King Hooligan
Ambassador Bourbon - To The Court Of Pazmania
The Courtier - To The Court Of Pazmania

King Alto - King Of Alettas
Princess Leilani - Only Child Of King Alto
Marsha Moss - Governess To Princess Leilani
Colonel Drayton - King Alto's Commander Of Guards
The White Servant - To King Alto
The Old Jailor - Frederic's Prison Guard

Major Reynolds - Officer To Frederic
The Young Lieutenant - Officer To Frederic
Colonel Drayton - Officer To King Alto
General Rudolph - Officer To Edmund
Colonel Hale - Officer to King Hooligan

Monsignor Saint Pierre - At The Abbey Of Trent
Miguel - A Shepard Boy
Father Francis - Priest At Edmund's Wake
Tarsus - The Deceased Tagolon

James Thaddeus Cobb - Captain Of The Ship Albatross

CAST OF CHARACTERS

Count Darby - Friend To Edmund
Big Red - Lead Mutineer On The Albatross
Other Mutineers - Ripcan, First Sailor, Second Sailor

A Foot Soldier – To King Frederic
Pella – Pazmanian Friend To Edmund
Thimble And Thread - Edmund's Hired Assassins
The Old Woman - Warns Frederic Of Robbers
Tom Hutchins - Frederic's Stable Boy
Rosalind - Jasmine's Girlfriend

The Tree Of Life
The Sword Of Tarsus
The Black Dragon

BOOK ONE

War Looms On The Horizon

All of the Lords and Barons were summoned
To Longhengren Castle, for the purpose of
Deciding what could be done about the war,
Which hung over the country of Arden like
Dark storm clouds prior to the apocalypse,
Making thunder, lightning, wind, and rain.
At this moment they were all assembled in
The great hall, when a magistrate came in
To focus their attention on King Frederic,
Who entered the room with blasts from the
Trumpets and much fanfare as is customary
Before taking a seat on the golden throne.

Without any delay in the proceedings, the
King spoke to all those present, and said,
"Thank you all for coming on short notice.
I know that many of you here had to leave
Travel and businesses, farms and families.
But you'll see that my reason warrants it.
No doubt you've heard the ambassador from
Pazmania was unhappy with our most recent
Decision to deny Pazmania access to fruit
From the Tree of Life, that we believe to
Be ours, since it was recently discovered
Growing on property that belongs to Arden.

We don't blame the Pazmanians for wanting
This fruit, since the valley where it was
Found lies on a border with their country,
And because whoever eats of this fruit is
Frequently healed from every disease, and
Brought back from the edge of death, even.
Nevertheless, it's my solemn duty as King
To protect the people of Arden and defend
Its valuable treasures; for this reason I
Have ordered each of you to raise an army
To stop the bold aggression from Pazmania,
Which hurries to capture the Tree of Life."

Right after they heard King Frederic speak,
Each one of the Barons knelt at the throne
And then made a pledge to raise a thousand
Soldiers, plus pay for all their equipment,
Which swelled the ranks of the army, until
Its strength measured in tens of thousands.
But many were still not satisfied, because
The King's brother, Edmund, did not attend
The meeting and had gone a hunting instead.
Wanting to know the truth, why this was so,
Some old friends of King Frederic drew him
Aside into a quiet corner for consultation.

General Killarney spoke first, "Edmund had
Better have a good reason for being absent.
Many Barons question his faith and loyalty."
King Frederic confessed he didn't know why,
"I suggest we hurry over to Windermere and
Give Edmund a chance to explain the reason."
Later that same evening, as Lord Dune rode
Beside General Killarney and King Frederic,
On the way to Windermere Castle, Lord Dune
Painted Edmund with a better light, saying,
"Last week the air was raw, cold, and damp.
Maybe Edmund lies sick in bed with a fever."

But an hour later, Lord Dune would abandon
This opinion, when they entered the castle
And looked inside of the great hall, where
A party of revelers laughed and held hands,
When they went in circles around the floor,
Dancing to music being played by musicians.
Making this situation worse, Edmund danced
On top of a table, his maleness exposed to
The ladies, after he had lost his garments
In a game of dice, and all his modesty too,
After having drunk a quantity of red wines
Fit enough for an old Roman bacchanal orgy.

Acting at once, King Frederic broke up the
Party, telling the heralds to announce his
Presence, which they did by blowing a loud
Blaring sound on the trumpets; immediately,
The crowd awoke to panic, and everyone put
On some clothes, not necessarily their own.
Everyone that is except Edmund, who picked
Up a table cloth to hide his private parts.
Now, as King Frederic crossed on the floor,
Followed by his entourage, Edmund tried to
Turn this into a joke by draping the table
Cloth over his shoulder, like a Roman toga.

But, neither King Frederic, nor the others,
Were amused, when they stopped in front of
Edmund, and then saw him raise his hand in
The air, from an imitation of Mark Anthony,
And heard him quote, "Ladies and gentlemen,
Lend me your ears, for mine have gone deaf
From listening to musicians, whose drunken
Songs sent me reeling with their cacophony."
Suddenly, laughter rippled in the ballroom.
This was followed by hecklers in the crowd,
Made up of many Pazmanians, some Ardenians,
All young, all wealthy, all of noble class.

"Ladies and gentiles, let me introduce you
To my brother, Frederic, who as first born,
And only two years older than me, is given
The right to become King of Arden, whereas
I who am born last must play second fiddle,
All on account of a mere accident of birth,"
Edmund said, encouraged by the applause of
The crowd. But, not everyone felt pleased.
General Killarney, for one, became enraged,
And said, "You have drunk too many cups of
Wine; show respect for the King, or you'll
Quickly feel the sharp prick from my sword."

It was a well known fact General Killarney
And Edmund hated each other; the old noble
Soldier lived discipline; the young prince
Loved freedom from restraint. Soon Edmund
Made a joke, saying, "Killarney, women who
Know say my sword's bigger than your sword."
To demonstrate this Edmund placed his hand
In between his legs and then slowly raised
The table cloth; suddenly the crowd roared
And applauded; Edmund had proved his point.
But General Killarney felt insulted and he
Quickly drew his sword to defend his honor.

However, King Frederic was able to prevent
Violence just by saying, "Patience General,
We have not come here to start any trouble.
Put up your sword." Right afterward, King
Frederic said to Edmund, "Your army should
Have mustered out, today, as per my orders,
Which were sent to you at the same time as
All of the Barons. Did you receive a copy?"
Edmund nodded his head, and said, "Brother,
Hear my explanation; I simply forgot about
The date, thinking it later on in the week.
Tell me the council's decision; do we make

Peace with Pazmania, or do we march to the
Border and fight over the Tree of Life? I
Have been told by my friends from Pazmania
To learn the King's desire on this subject."
So King Frederic said, "We'll defend Arden
And the Tree of Life, if this is necessary."
"Are you listening, Pella?" Edmund shouted.
"I may have to kill you in combat tomorrow."
"Then live life today," Pella said, joking.
But King Frederic was serious, and said to
Edmund, "Will you defend our children, our
Wives, and our homes from enemies of Arden?"

There was a brief pause, as though silence
Alone can convict Edmund of some falsehood.
General Killarney grew impatient, and said,
"Edmund, I've never known you to speak the
Truth if lies can better serve the purpose.
How much money have your Pazmanian friends
Paid you to spy on Arden in this shameless
Way?" Quickly, Edmund lost his temper; he
Jumped down from the table and then yelled,
"Leave my friends alone, Killarney; you've
Got the brains of a pig whose keen nose is
Good to sniff out trifles, I mean truffles."

Suddenly, King Frederic stepped in between
Them. Raising his hand, he said to Edmund,
"Your absence from the muster today caused
Some to question your loyalty to the crown.
You could put their fears to rest, telling
Us, here and now, you will bring your army."
"Why of course, dear brother," Edmund said,
"I will bring my army first thing tomorrow.
You can count on me to fight Arden's enemy,
No matter if they be real or imagined ones.
But don't set me next to General Killarney,
Since I just might cut out his evil tongue."

"That's enough!" King Frederic said, as he
Struggled to keep these two headstrong men
From coming to blows. "Your place will be
Beside me, as befits a brother to the King.
Now, since the hour is late, I will return
With my retinue to fair Longhengren Castle."
Later, as Edmund sat musing in his chamber,
He said, "I'll go if just to see the cause
Of so much fuss; I don't give a damn about
This war; but I must see this Tree of Life
Which fires up the imagination of men, who
Desire fruit and are willing to die for it."

Bright and early in the morning, while the
Sun rode over the sky like a fiery chariot
Above thousands of tents, closely encamped
Near Longhengren Castle, General Killarney
Deplored Edmund's absence, when he scoffed,
And said, by way of complaint to Lord Dune,
"It is as I told you; I've no trust in the
King's brother, Edmund, whose pledge means
Nothing at all; since he failed to show up
With his army, I win the bet, and you need
To pay me my golden ducat." But Lord Dune
Said to him, "Wait, the day is still young.

There's time for Edmund to appear with his
Army." But later, when it was around noon,
With still no signs that Edmund would come,
Lord Dune advised King Frederic, by saying,
"It would be unwise to wait another moment.
Our small garrison that guards the Tree of
Life would soon fall to a determined enemy.
I beseech your majesty, give the order now.
Let our legions begin their long march; in
The event Edmund comes later, his army may
Play catch up on the road." But to all of
This King Frederic said, "Patience, let us

Wait another hour." Soon, someone shouted,
"Look, a large dust cloud rises in the sky,
High above the hill. It may be Edmund who
Marches from Windermere, bringing his army."
So everyone watched, while two riders came
Within sight, bearing Edmund's olive crest.
They advanced swiftly, rode over the knoll,
And soon came to where King Frederic stood,
Surrounded with his lords. It was Malcolm,
The most famous Knight errant in the realm,
Who approached King Frederic, and said, "I
Bring terrible news, sire. Edmund is dead."

"Dead," a shocked King Frederic stammered.
"How can it be? When we departed, Edmund
Was in good spirits." So Malcolm replied,
"Forgive my plain language; I'm a soldier
Who has none of the good manners at court."
When King Frederic said, "Start any story
From the beginning, and more shall follow,"
Malcolm replied, "I will heed your advice.
While on the way here, Edmund lingered to
Shoot a wild boar with an arrow. At once,
The wounded creature ran off to hide in a
Swamp, where tall reeds grow in profusion.

Edmund then told General Rudolph that the
Army should continue marching and that he
Would catch up with him, after he entered
In the swamp all alone, and he had killed
The creature, hidden back among the trees.
Although Edmund was a skillful hunter, he
Was caught by surprise when the wild boar
Quickly raced through the undergrowth and
Cut his horse on the front leg, using one
Of its sharp tusks. More frightened than
Hurt, the horse reared up on its haunches,
Throwing Edmund onto the ground, where he

Bumped his head on a rock, which rendered
Him unconscious. Edmund moaned pitifully,
While his eyes rolled up in their sockets.
But Edmund answered not our pleas, and so
We rolled him in a chair made of blankets
And brought him back to Windermere Castle
And then carried him to his private rooms,
Where he lay still, not moving on the bed,
While the Physician held up to his lips a
Silver mirror to see if it created a mist.
Alas, this Physician saw no signs of life,
And sighed, before he told us he had died.

Soon, after Malcolm had finished his story,
King Frederic quieted his anxious officers,
Saying, "Edmund and I no longer loved each
Other as brothers ought; but I'm obligated
To attend his funeral. You're needed more
At the Tree of Life than at Edmund's grave.
While I'm away, General Killarney shall be
In command. Swear you'll take orders from
Him just as if you had gotten them from me."
"We swear, by God and things Holy, to obey
General Killarney," all of the Barons said.
"I'll return in a few days," King Frederic

Said, before he rode away in the direction
Of Windermere Castle, accompanied by a few
Guards. He arrived at the castle, just at
Sunset, while trees cast long dark shadows
Over a highway, a stone bridge, and a moat.
After stopping in the courtyard, they were
Met by a Franciscan Priest, Father Francis,
Who showed King Frederic the chamber where
Edmund now lay in state inside of a coffin.
To his surprise, some Pazmanians were here,
All friends of Edmund; walking up to kneel
Down in front of the coffin, King Frederic

Bowed his head and closed his eyes, hoping
To appear reverent; however, King Frederic
Lacked true faith, and only showed respect
By reciting those prayers spoken by Father
Francis. The Pazmanians expected the King
To speak the praises of Edmund in a eulogy
And were shocked to see he remained silent,
Even as they all left the chamber together.
The Priest kept vigil throughout the night.
When King Frederic woke up at dawn, inside
A room in the castle, he heard a noise and
Then found the Priest in the hall, sobbing.

"Why do you stand by my door at this hour?"
King Frederic asked. When Father Francis
Continued to weep without answering, King
Frederic shook him by both shoulders, and
Said, "Come on man find your tongue; tell
Me what happened before I sound the alarm."
Wiping away his tears, the Priest blurted,
"Forgive me, sire, I bring fantastic news.
Your brother, Edmund, who we thought dead,
Now lives and breathes again, either by a
Miracle or from sorcery, I know not which."
So, King Frederic asked, "How can this be?"

I felt his cold hand; I saw his face gray
With the mask of death." The Priest said,
"It happened as I knelt and prayed before
His coffin, then glanced up to see Edmund
Staring at me, with red eyes like a devil.
He asked for water, and drank two glasses,
Saying Hell felt hot, and smelled foul as
Rotten eggs. How I hated his cruel laugh.
You're a good Priest, he said, mocking me.
You shall never know Hell! Then suddenly,
He yelled, cursed God and everything holy,
And told me to leave the chamber, at once.

Immediately afterward, I came to stand in
Front of your door, where I hesitated and
Dared not to knock, because I felt afraid
Of bringing news to you both good and bad.
It was then that you heard me sobbing and
Then discovered me in a fit of depression."
King Frederic thought over this situation.
When he spoke again, momentarily, he said,
"I've heard that these strange things can
Happen and am now eager to ask my brother
All about his near death experience. Come,
I want you at my side when I question him."

At first, Father Francis was reluctant to
Go along with King Frederic and then show
Him the chamber, where Edmund got dressed
In his military uniform without his valet
There to assist him. But, Father Francis
Remembered the Lord, who gave him courage
To lead the way there, and he showed King
Frederic that chamber where Edmund sat in
A chair, pulling on his tall riding boots.
But, as soon as Edmund saw Father Francis,
He said, with a vile curse, "What is this
Priest doing here? All Priests are pests!"

Then it was King Frederic's turn to speak,
And he said, "This Priest is here because
I have asked him. You were dead but live
Again, and for this we thank God, and His
Only son, Jesus. Father Francis tells me
You went to Hell, and there you saw Satan."
Now looking at King Frederic, Edmund said,
"For once, this zealot has told the truth.
But as for Jesus, there are many good men
Who came to preach to the world, men like
Buddha, and Mohammed, and Pazmanizell the
Pazmanian. They are all equal in my eyes.

But enough, I grow weary of religion; let
Us go and join our armies that are camped
In the Valley of Death." Just then, King
Frederic asked, in surprise, "How can you
Know the secret passwords? You were dead!"
"Satan told me," Edmund replied, casually.
Without further delay, Edmund walked from
The castle clear out to the horse stables.
When all alone, Edmund said in reflection,
"How can I tell my brother that Satan has
Promised me his crown, and untimely death,
If I do only obey, serve, and worship him?"

Two weeks later, in the company of Edmund
And his guards, King Frederic came to the
Valley of Death, and saw a Pazmanian army
Was camped on one side of the border, and
The Ardenian army was camped on the other,
While the Tree of Life grew in the middle.
That afternoon, since Edmund was eager to
Look on the Tree of Life, they went there
To eat of its fruit, that is everyone but
Edmund who described it in this way, "The
Fruit has the sweet sickening odor of God,
Like overly ripened pears in the sunshine."

Now that he knew it can heal all diseases,
King Frederic said, "The benefits of this
Fruit should be shared among every nation.
I will request that we begin negotiations
With Pazmania, first." True to his words,
King Frederic invited Pazmanian delegates
To a conference, which opened discussions
To decide on a fair distribution of fruit.
These talks went so well in the beginning,
King Frederic decided this good cause for
A celebration, by having a ballroom dance,
Followed next day by a tournament of arms.

This brought favor from all of the ladies,
Who could dress up in the newest fashions,
And from all of the gentlemen and Knights,
Who could parade with their military pomp,
Then perform with all manner of skills in
The joust, at archery, and even swordplay.
Since it was declared only the Knights of
Arden will participate within these games,
Edmund invited the entire delegation from
Pazmania to sit in his booth, so they can
Watch Malcolm, his fabulous Knight errant,
Meet all challengers, he being a champion.

King Frederic liked to dance, with most of
The pretty ladies, regardless if they were
Married. When one dance ended and another
Began, King Frederic noticed the beautiful
Kathleen, Malcolm's wife, looking right at
Him, her blue eyes like stars in the night.
As the current dance had ended, and before
The next one began, King Frederic left the
Side of Lord Dune's wife, and then went to
Take Kathleen's hand, and then lead her in
The next waltz played by the six musicians.
First to speak, King Frederic asked, "Have

You been to see the beautiful Tree of Life?"
Her answer surprised him. "Yes," Kathleen
Said, "I went yesterday afternoon, when it
Was reported that doves were seen roosting
In the Tree, singing hallowed church songs."
As their conversation went on in this vein,
General Killarney made this remark to Lord
Dune, who stood on the sidelines, watching,
"Should the King dance with that woman who
Obviously has a wanton lust in her manners?"
"I feel certain, it must be Edmund's doing,"
Lord Dune said, in a moral tone. "He's to

Blame for introducing her to King Frederic."
"You can be sure of it," General Killarney,
Said, disparagingly, with his sour stomach.
"If a thing smells bad Edmund must be near."
Then Lord Dune went on, saying, "Just look
What close friends Edmund is to all of the
Pazmanians; why he practically rubs elbows
With Ambassador Bourbon, whose front teeth
Remind me of a large rat who eats cabbages.
The King should not have put Edmund's army
Next to his own in the field; Edmund can't
Be trusted; his ambition is out of control."

Then General Killarney offered his opinion,
"Nothing good can come from low beginnings.
The King is an embarrassment to himself by
Admiring this woman, whose desire is plain.
She uses the King to climb a social ladder
In order to gain influence with the nobles."
Lord Dune agreed, "You are right of course.
But what can be done at so late a juncture?
Stop them, and you risk the displeasure of
The King." General Killarney watched them
Dancing for a moment, and then said, "This
Exceeds my patience; I'll put an end to it."

Without telling anyone his plan especially
Lord Dune, General Killarney went onto the
Balcony, where he spoke to Lord Dune's son,
Chester Dune, some young hot head, who was
Known for acting on impulse, and then said,
"I have a favor to ask, will you oblige me?"
As he had hoped he would, this officer who
Had only a few soft downy hairs growing on
His face, replied, "Yes of course, our two
Families have been friends for a long time.
What is it?" Just then, General Killarney
Said, "The King makes a fool of himself by

Dancing with a woman who acts like a whore.
Will you be so kind as to break them apart?
I would do it, but my wounded leg prevents
Me from joining in the dance." Looking at
His mahogany cane, Chester Dune gave a nod,
And then asked, "What is this woman's name?"
"Kathleen, wife of Malcolm, a proud Knight
Errant who currently fights for the King's
Brother, Edmund." So Chester Dune replied,
"I've longed for a chance to fight Malcolm
And then knock him off from his high horse.
I know what to do. Leave everything to me."

Right after talking with General Killarney,
Chester Dune went into the ballroom, where
King Frederic danced a waltz with Kathleen,
And tapping him on his shoulder, he cut in
Front of King Frederic to become her dance
Partner, inline with the custom of the day.
Soon afterward, Chester Dune paused in the
Dance and said to Kathleen, with arrogance,
"All eyes were on you when you danced with
King Frederic. Many find it inappropriate
And say things that would shame your honor."
Intrigued, Kathleen asked, "What things do

People say about me sir? I should be told."
Taking this opportunity, Chester Dune said,
"Madame, it's the opinion of many that you
Embarrass King Frederic by your attentions,
Which are like the wanton lusts of a whore.
My advice is this, stay away from the King."
In the belief Chester Dune had injured her
Reputation, Kathleen rushed over the floor
And told her husband Malcolm what happened.
Suddenly enraged by what he heard, Malcolm
Rushed over to find Chester Dune, and said,
"My wife informs me that you have insulted

Her reputation by comparing her to a whore!"
So Chester Dune said, "If your wife dances
With the King like a whore, is flirtatious
Like a whore, paints her face like a whore,
Reason will tell you, the woman is a whore!"
At once, Malcolm slapped Chester Dune hard
On the face with his hand. "Honor demands
That I have satisfaction!" Malcolm shouted.
"Meet me, at one o'clock tomorrow, so that
We will joust, not with blunt weapons used
By amateurs, but with normal battle lances."
"Good!" Chester Dune said, and he went out.

So that next day, at the appointed hour of
One o'clock, in the afternoon, Malcolm and
Chester Dune waited patiently on horseback
For King Frederic to begin the games again.
The crowd was eager for the event to start.
However, in a moment King Frederic delayed
The event and made this comment in earnest,
"Instead of using lances with blunted ends,
They use pointed lances; this violates all
Of the rules." Immediately, King Frederic
Spoke to General Killarney, Lord Dune, and
His brother, Edmund, when he said, alarmed,

"I want to know who approved those weapons.
I feel as though I should stop the contest,
Before one Knight injures the other Knight."
But at that moment, General Killarney said,
"Let the joust resume; I think the contest
Shall boost morale among all of the troops."
Also, Lord Dune echoed a similar sentiment,
When he said, "The joust should be allowed
To begin on time since my son brings honor
To my family." When Edmund added, "I hope
Malcolm triumphs, for a patron like myself
Profits most from those who bet against me,"

King Frederic felt out voted by a majority
And then set aside his usual good judgment,
And signaled the judges to start the games.
At once, when the trumpets blared, the two
Knights lowered their lances, and galloped
Their big fiery steeds, from opposite ends.
In a few seconds, when they met each other
At the center of the gallery, Chester Dune
Broke a lance harmlessly against Malcolm's
Shield, whilst Malcolm's lance glanced off
His shield and drove the point in his neck
And through his throat, severing his spine.

Since Dame Rachael Dune hated violence of
Any kind, she refused to attend the games.
Instead she remained at home in her lodge,
Where two of her maids were in attendance,
Cynthia and Susanne, who tried everything
They knew how to calm her excessive worry.
But the noise and roar of the crowd which
Sat in the gallery upset her to the point
Her nerves began to unravel like the ball
Of yarn which slipped out of her hand and
Then rolled willy nilly across the carpet.
But Cynthia bent to pick up the ball, and

Returned the yarn to Dame Rachael who was
Thinking of last night, when she said, "I
Had a dream in which Chester fell injured."
Now talking to Cynthia, Dame Rachael said,
"Depart at once for the tournament; bring
Back in a hurry any news of my son's fate."
Doing what she had been told, Cynthia ran
To the tournament, and then soon returned.
Instantly, when seeing her quiet demeanor,
Dame Rachael felt the emotions of despair,
And said, "A very terrible thing happened.
You don't need to tell me, my son is dead!

A mother knows if her child is in trouble
Because we are tied together by a cord at
Birth." When Dame Rachael cried, Cynthia
Nodded her head, then said, "Chester fell,
Pierced by a lance in the neck. Mortally
Slain, he died and then gave up the ghost.
Lord Dune is having him carried here on a
Stretcher. I hurried ahead, so you could
Wait for them; they'll be here any minute.
Lord Dune's heart broke in two as Chester
Looked up at him one last time and smiled,
Then shut his eyes, and in his arms, died."

When Dame Rachael Dune heard those bearers
Coming inside of the house, at that moment,
Carrying the body of her dead son, Chester
Dune, she soon dashed out into the hallway
And then paused to lean over the stretcher,
Where she cradled his head with both hands,
Saying, "Infant, let me kiss thy warm lips
One last time before ye lie in a cold tomb.
How often have I rocked thee to sleep upon
My lap and sung thee lullabies when dreams
Were bad or kissed thee on thy bumped head
To take away all thy pain, countless times?"

At that moment, Dame Rachael turned to her
Husband, Lord Dune, who she blamed for her
Son's death, saying, "It is your fault our
Darling boy has courted death like a lover.
You've encouraged him to take up the joust.
Tell me the name of the man who killed him."
Immediately Lord Dune grew angry, and said,
To everyone present, and especially to his
Bold wife, "You've only spoiled the boy by
Pampering him from the time he was a child.
But in spite of this, Chester became a man,
Who fought and then died as a brave Knight."

Cynthia, silent all of this time, now said
To her old Dame, "While I was there, I saw
The Knight who has slain your poor Chester.
The Knight goes by the name of Sir Malcolm.
The lady to whom I spoke told me the joust
Happened because Chester insulted his wife,
Who compromised the reputation of the King."
Suddenly Lord Dune lost patience, and said,
"Who will believe a servant girl? Get out
Of my way! I will honor my son, by taking
Him in the bedroom, where we will wash and
Dress him, and prepare his body for burial."

About an hour later, King Frederic arrived
In the carriage, along with his Physicians,
Who had gone to the Tree of Life, and then
Returned with some fruit, contained in the
Purple velvet bag, they made into a potion
And brought to restore Chester Dune's life.
Soon they were joined by a second carriage,
Which contained more passengers, including
Malcolm and Kathleen, who were with Edmund
And the delegate from Pazmania, Ambassador
Bourbon, who had all come there to support
The notion that the fruit can work wonders.

King Frederic believed it would be best if
Everyone stayed outside, while two doctors
Or Physicians went on into the house, this
To lessen overcrowding in the same bedroom,
Where family members and even the servants
Were praying all around Chester Dune's bed.
Outside, when they walked through the yard,
Edmund fell into conversation with Malcolm
And Ambassador Bourbon, who said, speaking
To Malcolm, as Edmund listened in, "By God,
You showed rare skills in the joust, today.
Would you consider fighting for my team in

Pazmania?" But Malcolm declined to accept
Ambassador Bourbon's offer to make lots of
Money there, saying to him, "King Frederic
Forbids us to visit Pazmania due to all of
The unrest between our two nations." This
Is when Edmund said, "The King will change
His mind, when peace is restored to normal.
However, if I were you, I would leave soon,
Until things have settled down, once again.
Lord Dune can make your life uncomfortable
If you stay." But Malcolm said, "Arden is
My home; I've no intention of leaving here."

Meanwhile, King Frederic and Kathleen, who
Had gone further on down the path together,
Soon vanished out of sight behind the barn,
From where Kathleen peered around a corner
To see if any of the others were following.
"They are all up near the house," Kathleen
Said, whispering it in King Frederic's ear.
Just then King Frederic did what few would
Dare to believe: he embraced Kathleen with
Both arms, and then kissed her on the lips.
Being in love, they kissed again and again,
Until Kathleen asked, when pushing him off,

"I hate meeting in secret; sooner or later,
Everybody will find out that we are lovers.
What happens then? Six months have passed,
Since you asked Cardinal Vidal to annul my
Marriage, so that we two may legally marry.
Why does a vassal defer answering his King,
When a divorce from Malcolm brings freedom?"
King Frederic groaned, and then said, "Not
Even the King can tell Cardinal Vidal what
He must do; and besides, I was told by him
That this decision must come from the Pope,
Whose office is in Rome; try to be patient."

Right then, Kathleen took King Frederic by
The hand, and then forced him to touch the
Small round bump that grew within her womb.
"This baby that you feel will not wait for
The Cardinal to make a decision. You must
Find a good solution, before we are shamed."
King Frederic thought for a moment, and he
Said, "I plan to send Malcolm to the front.
There, he shall be locked up in prison for
The rest of his life. It shall be told he
Was missing in action, captured, or killed."
"Well, be quick about it," Kathleen warned.

Right then, they heard the voice of one of
The Physicians who called telling everyone
To come into the house and see the miracle
That God has done for his servant, Chester
Dune, who now lies awake in bed, asking to
See Malcolm, and all of the others as well.
Funny, who should appear around the corner
Of the shelter where they stood, just then,
But this Malcolm, husband of Kathleen, who
Nearly caught her in the act of infidelity,
And yet remained clueless of their romance.
"They want you to go inside," Malcolm said.

King Frederic was surprised to see Malcolm,
But was calm as a cucumber, as he searched
Malcolm's face for suspicion. Relieved to
See there was none, King Frederic breathed
Normal again, and then said, "Come, let us
To the house and see this miracle together."
On the way back to the house, Edmund spoke,
Whispering low so no one could hear, "Wait
Ambassador, I'd speak with you on a matter
Of importance." After everyone had passed
Them on their way to the house, Ambassador
Bourbon said to Edmund, "What matter is so

Secret you have to hide it from the others?"
Edmund replied, hooking his arm around the
Ambassador's arm, "I've a certain proposal
To make, one concerning the fruit from the
Tree of Life; King Frederic plans to cheat
The Pazmanians out of their fair share, by
Offering a mere ten percent. On the other
Hand, if I were to be made King, with help
From my Pazmanian friends, I would take no
More than my equal share, that is one half."
"I will tell my King," the Ambassador said.
"Let us go in, before we arouse suspicions."

So they all crowded into the small bedroom
To hear a mysterious story by Chester Dune,
Who welcomed everyone there, and then said,
"But where is Malcolm, the man who slew me?"
Kathleen answered him, saying, "My husband
Is in the hall, too embarrassed to see you."
"Then tell him to come in. I've something
Important to say, and I want everyone here,"
Chester Dune said. But, no one there felt
Surprised to see the Dunes were distraught
When Malcolm entered the bedroom and stood
By the bed, hanging his head down in shame.

Suddenly, Chester Dune said to Malcolm, "I
Hope you'll find forgiveness in your heart
For the awful things I said about Kathleen.
I should not have called her any bad names.
Please sit down, and take my hand in yours,
And then listen, while I tell my sad story."
Doing what he was asked, Malcolm swallowed
His pride, and reached out to take Chester
Dune's hand, just as he began to tell them
What happened, saying, " I died, I floated
In outer darkness, and I saw nothing there.
When I asked, what would become of my fate,

I immediately felt a sense of overwhelming
Love. In a brief moment, I now understood
This love had come from God, even though I
Was unable to see him, or locate a precise
Presence. As I peered into the dark abyss,
I saw what looked like thin silver strands,
Like a spider's web shimmering in sunlight.
Thus, I was held there, suspended in space,
Perhaps for an eternity. Then, I began to
Struggle free. I wished to search for God.
But, I was held fast by the silver strands,
Until, weak with exhaustion, I fell asleep."

Then Chester Dune paused for just a moment
To drink more from the glass that was half
Full of fruit juice; he felt better on the
Instant, and then continued to tell a tale
That greatly astonished the crowd, as they
Stood around his bed, listening to him say,
"I thought that I had died, just then, and
That at last I had journeyed toward Heaven.
But to my surprise, I was kneeling down on
A large boulder, and I wasn't alone; Jesus
Was there with me, hanging from that cross,
Exactly like on the day of his crucifixion.

Time seemed eternal here, as I watched his
Face dripping with sweat, blood, and tears.
Then I became afraid, knowing he was dying,
Not only for my sins; but, for the sins of
The world. When I started to weep, all of
A sudden, he said, 'Why do you weep for me?
Weep for all of those who hate me, and who
Curse my name, for they are the lost sheep,
And they shall be called the sons of Satan.'
Soon, a drop of his blood fell in my wound,
Where the lance had cut me; on the instant,
He healed me, I knew my sins were forgiven."

It was right then that Chester Dune paused
In his tale; on seeing how tired he looked,
The Physicians told everybody to leave the
Bedroom, because Chester needed more sleep.
So they shushed everyone outside like hens
In a barn yard. Once there, King Frederic
Drew Malcolm aside, and then said, "I wish
To send you on an important mission, which
Shall require you to spy on the Pazmanians.
You leave early tomorrow." Malcolm seemed
Surprised by this, but only said, "My wish
Is to serve my King. I'll go pack my bags."

When two weeks had passed, Kathleen again
Found herself in the private chamber with
King Frederic, who admired her beauty and
Watched, as she removed layers of clothes,
Then dropped each one down onto the floor,
Until she stood in only her undergarments.
But this time, when King Frederic came up
To embrace her, Kathleen stepped backward
A little ways, and then said, "I spoke to
Dame Rachael, who has confided in me that
There are rumors, which insinuate Malcolm
Is dead. I want you to tell me the truth."

King Frederic paused for a moment, before
He said to Kathleen, "I've heard the same
Rumors. Apparently, something went wrong
With my plan. My guards were supposed to
Make Malcolm their prisoner, not kill him."
Now Kathleen said, "I want to believe you.
But, how do I know if you speak the truth?"
So King Frederic said, massaging Kathleen
On the arm, "One soldier survived, and he
Will speak to the senators at the council.
He's the last person to see Malcolm alive.
Why not come to the council, and then sit

In the antechamber, holding the door ajar,
So that you may hear the truth, with your
Own ears; in this way you need not depend
On my words alone, but have an eyewitness."
Suddenly, feeling less doubtful, Kathleen
Draped her arms over King Frederic's neck.
"I want us to be happy," Kathleen said in
A sorrowful voice. "But the machinations
Of the whole world do conspire against us."
King Frederic then used a finger to touch
Her lips, and said, "Quiet, we shall find
Happiness in love. Come, let me kiss you."

When all of the Ardenian senators attended
The forum that day at one in the afternoon,
They listened intently to the one and only
Survivor from that massacre, a common foot
Infantry who described how twenty soldiers
Died, along with Malcolm the Knight errant.
"Malcolm had sent us out on patrol to make
Certain the Pazmanians had not crossed our
Border," the Corporal said, "but instantly,
We were attacked by two hundred Pazmanians,
Who had waited in ambush, and out of sight,
Behind the boulders." Here, King Frederic

Interrupted the Corporal for a moment, and
Then said, "Did Malcolm at any time during
The expedition order his soldiers to cross
Over the border into Pazmania?" Answering
Him, the Corporal said, "No, sire, Malcolm
Never told us to go across, I'm sure of it.
Once we'd been surprised by the Pazmanians,
Malcolm made us form in a circle, and then
Stand on top of a large hill in the forest.
Here, we defended each other when attacked,
And the enemy paid dearly with their lives.
But even Malcolm, with all of his fighting

Skills, fell when receiving four arrows in
His body. Although we fought courageously,
The Pazmanians, who greatly outnumbered us,
Killed every last soldier; I alone escaped
By lying face down in the dirt, pretending
To be dead, as Pazmanian soldiers stripped
Us of all possessions, including our boots.
I waited until dark, when I felt sure they
Had gone away. Only then did I feel brave
Enough to stand and then walk back to camp.
Although three days on foot, I'd volunteer
To go at once, and bring their bodies home."

Now, the eyewitness took his seat and the
Ambassador from Pazmania rose to his feet.
Soon as he was called on by King Frederic,
He said, "Esteemed senators, I shall tell
What happened on that day, as it was told
To me by Colonel Hale, our senior officer,
Who led the charge on the Ardenian troops.
According to Colonel Hale and some others,
The Ardenians came to spy on our position.
However, when Colonel Hale had asked them
To withdraw within the prescribed borders,
He said the Ardenian soldiers, which were

Around twenty, began an unprovoked attack.
Naturally, he responded from self defense."
King Frederic thought the Ambassador lied.
But he let him go on without interruption.
After he had finished, King Frederic said,
"Does the right honorable Ambassador wish
To say something more about this incident?"
"No, not right now," that Ambassador said,
"But I'd like to make a few final remarks."
"You may start when you feel ready," King
Frederic said. Just then, the Ambassador
Would insult the whole council, by saying,

"Please believe me when I tell all of you
That the people of Pazmania have thus far
Shown great restraint. But, our patience
Shall not last forever. The Tree of Life
Grows within an area that's been disputed
For generations. We feel the fruit is as
Much ours as it is yours, and we want our
Fair share, not just a measly ten percent."
This angered the senators who shouted and
Refused to restore order. Feeling he had
No other choice but to beat a gavel, King
Frederic said, "This meeting is adjourned!"

When this meeting was over, King Frederic
Stood up, and went out to the antechamber
To find Kathleen, and on the instant they
Met, they greeted one another with a kiss.
"You have heard the story," King Frederic
Said, "Do I still deserve your suspicions?"
Looking up with those intense indigo eyes
Right at King Frederic, Kathleen imagined
That his handsome face had told the truth.
"I believe you," Kathleen said, as if she
Wanted to apologize, "but I doubt if that
Pazmanian Ambassador is telling the truth."

"I agree, the Ambassador salts his speech
With lies." After a pause, Kathleen said,
"The man in the witness chair has claimed
My husband, Malcolm, was killed in action.
Is he dead?" King Frederic nodded. "Yes.
In a few days, my search party will bring
Malcolm's body home for the state funeral.
The people will expect you to observe our
Custom of mourning by wearing black gowns.
We must wait a year and then we can marry."
"No, I won't wear those awful black gowns,
Or wear long sad faces to please everyone!"

Kathleen was upset, and ranted. "Neither
Will I wait longer than one month; I will
Start counting the days after his funeral.
Malcolm and I no longer loved one another.
I shall not stand by and let his long arm
Reach out from the grave to spoil the day
On which we wed." King Frederic realized
Kathleen could be stubborn and he avoided
An argument with her by agreeing to marry
On any day she chose. This made Kathleen
Very happy, and for the rest of the month
She talked nothing else but nuptial plans.

When Edmund failed to hear from Ambassador
Bourbon and remained unsure whether or not
King Hooligan would agree to send his army
To help him fight the Ardenians, he looked
To hire two assassins, who would kill King
Frederic in the church, on his wedding day.
Edmund went at night to visit the brothels
And bars, always located in the worst part
Of any town, until he was able to find two
Dark characters who agreed to be assassins,
If they were paid a reward with gold coins,
After they had carried out this dirty deed.

Edmund then gave them careful instructions,
And told them to wait in their aisle seats,
Until the time King Frederic would pass by,
When they were to jump up, then strike him
With daggers. But like with lots of plans,
Even rehearsed ones, events easily go awry,
When an unpredictable part of the equation
Appears. In this case, it was the sixteen
Year old cousin of King Frederic, Giovanni
Younger, who was slain for heroics when he
Stepped in between the assassins, and gave
The time necessary for King Frederic to go

Hide in the sacristy, a sanctuary upstairs,
From where he looked down over the balcony
And saw Giovanni lying on the marble floor,
In a pool of blood. Soon the congregation
Ran toward the exits, and emptied from the
Cathedral, like some voice had yelled fire.
Then afterward, the whole city was alarmed,
When soldiers searched from house to house
And checked near every waterway, and under
Every bridge, also through every city park,
All night long, until they were frustrated,
Because the assassins had soon disappeared.

Immediately after this event, Edmund went
To look for King Frederic in the sacristy,
Where Physicians bandaged his wounded arm,
And regretting that his brother yet lived,
Edmund said, "I leave at once to hunt for
Two assassins, who did this heinous crime.
There may be more; I hope to bring all of
Them to justice." So then, King Frederic
Said, "If you do, Edmund, I will thank my
Brother, and then give him a great reward."
So Edmund left the cathedral, with a band
Of trustworthy guards, and then rode from

Town, heading for some wilderness highway,
And the place where he had agreed to meet
The two assassins, who were hiding inside
Of an old cottage, back in the deep woods.
Stopping in front of the old cottage door,
Edmund yelled to the two assassins, using
Their fictional names and aliases, saying,
"Thimble and Thread, this is Edmund, come
Out, I only want to talk; don't be afraid."
Immediately the door opened a small crack,
And then swung wide open, as two men came
Out and then glanced nervously about them.

"The boy jumped in the way," Thimble said,
"And he received blows meant for the King,
Who I know I cut on the arm with a dagger.
We think we should get part of our reward
Now, and the rest when we murder the King."
Edmund, knowing to leave behind witnesses
Would be a mistake, shouted to his guards,
"I don't reward failure; kill these fools!"
On realizing they were deceived by Edmund,
The men ran to save their lives; but only
Reached far as the door, before they fell,
All of sudden, struck by a hail of arrows.

Then, while Edmund brought both assassins
To Longhengren Castle, their bodies slung
Over the backs of horses, it came to pass
Edmund met a rider along the road who had
Come to deliver a message from Ambassador
Bourbon. Quickly, Edmund read the letter,
Which said, 'King Hooligan gladly accepts
Your plan whose details we can discuss in
Camp when you have returned to the valley.'
Eagerly stuffing the letter in his pocket,
Edmund rode on to Longhengren Castle, and
Showed the men to King Frederic, who said,

On seeing this one with a long cheek scar
And that one with a blind eye, "Well done,
Edmund, you've caught the assassins; take
This purse of gold coins as an expression
Of my gratitude." Edmund, believing that
He can create more mischief, said to King
Frederic, "I see no reason why you should
Leave Longhengren to take up your command,
Since General Killarney and Lord Dune and
Myself are capable of commanding the army.
Once there, I'll send you plenty of fruit,
So as to heal your wounded arm, instantly.

You can use this time to grow in strength;
And besides, you should share a honeymoon,
In bed with your wife you so recently wed."
King Frederic felt relieved, and said, "I
Accept this kind offer, Edmund. I'm glad
We two brothers have become friends again."
Later on that same night, when Edmund was
Alone in the parlor, he said in amusement,
"Frederic takes the bait and will be away
During the battle for Arden. I only wish
I could see his face, when he learns, too
Late, his army fell in defeat without him."

When Edmund arrived in the Valley of Death,
Just a week later, he spoke with his Chief
Of Staff, General Rudolph, concerning last
Minute details of his devious plan, saying,
"Does everyone have instructions to follow
When the Pazmanians approach our positions?"
Fully confident they would win this battle,
General Rudolph said, "I told the officers
To turn and attack Lord Dune in the center,
While the Pazmanians attack from the front.
In this way, we quickly collapse Lord Dune,
Then throw him back upon General Killarney."

Edmund tapped the map with his riding whip,
And then said, "Excellent, much happens in
The next few hours. Very soon, fate shall
Reverse our fortunes; I will be victorious,
And then wear the King's crown, signifying
That I, the new monarch, am ruler of Arden,
Whereas my brother, Frederic, shall become
Yesterday's King, and must perforce bow to
Me, having been made my prisoner in chains.
Fate is often fickle, but even fools shall
Seem wise, when they surrender their power
To wiser men, who make them unfit for rule.

Some believe, naively, the goodness of men
Shall forever stay triumphant in the world.
But I will show them wrong is always right.
I hope you agree, General Rudolph," Edmund
Said, just before he smiled like a villain.
"Yes of course, only the strongest survive."
"I'm pleased that we share similar beliefs,"
Edmund said. "General Rudolph, a talented
Fellow like yourself shall do well in this
New order. First, we must win this battle.
Let us now join our troops, who shall lead
Us to victory, and King Frederic to defeat."

When drawn up in battle formation, General
Killarney left his place on the right wing
To talk with Lord Dune who held the center.
"The fog lies over the valley this morning,"
Lord Dune said, "Should the enemy risk an
Attack, we may not see them coming in time."
"Some days have passed since we last heard
From King Frederic, who should be here now
To resume command," General Killarney said.
"What reason keeps him from doing his duty?"
"The King has sent word that he'll be late.
His wound causes him pain," Lord Dune said.

"This isn't his only reason for being late,"
Lord Dune continued, with a nervous twitch.
"I believe a second reason was due in part
Because he and his wife are newly wed, and
They frolic together in between the sheets."
Just then, General Killarney lost patience,
And shouted, "The woman ruins his judgment!
He should be here before the battle begins!"
"Have faith," Lord Dune went on, "that our
Army is victorious, with or without a King."
Just then, they saw ghost like apparitions
Appearing in the fog, marching toward them.

"Wait, what's this I see on our left flank?"
General Killarney asked, in surprise. "Do
I dare believe my eyes; Edmund deceives us,
And attacks simultaneously with Pazmanians?
By his orders, the soldiers in his command
Do deliver a mortal blow against your wing."
Observing chaos everywhere, Lord Dune said,
"Edmund now plays a traitor, damn his soul!
Look, the enemy charges, and coward like a
Whole army runs down the road, retreats as
If from a swarm of angry bees. We've lost
Everything, General. Quick, save yourself!"

When King Frederic realized that infection
Had swollen his arm, and that Edmund still
Had not sent the fruit, as he had promised,
He decided to cut short his stay, and ride
To the Valley of Death, escorted by guards,
To take command of the Ardenian army again.
But King Frederic became surprised, all of
A sudden, when he came along the road, and
Saw the army had been routed off the field,
Leaving dropped equipment behind for miles,
In its desperate effort to lighten burdens,
And keep just ahead of the advancing enemy.

Eventually, he passed groups of stragglers
Who were coming from the front, right near
The battle, which he heard in the distance.
Soon he saw some officers on the road, and
Halting them, King Frederic asked, "Why do
You retreat when the enemy gives us battle?"
At that moment one officer, Major Reynolds,
Who recognized King Frederic, said at once,
"Your evil brother, Edmund, does betray us
To the hated Pazmanians. You are not safe
On the road since our army has been routed."
So King Frederic replied, "Help me to turn

Our soldiers; we must rally them if we are
To push back the enemy and win our victory."
But try hard as they might to make a stand,
The soldiers ignored orders; some ran away
From King Frederic and all of his officers,
Fearing them even more than the Pazmanians.
When Major Reynolds saw that King Frederic
Was sick, he said, "Perhaps the Pazmanians
Have yet to surround the Tree of Life; its
Benevolent fruit may heal thy wound." And
To this King Frederic said, "Hurry up; I'm
Dying, the fruit is my last chance at life."

With Major Reynolds leading the way there,
They climbed steadily, until they reached
A place that overlooked the valley, where
They looked in wonder at the Tree of Life,
Which seemed to sparkle in the atmosphere,
Along with a rainbow arched high overhead.
Seeing that the enemy had not yet arrived,
Major Reynolds placed one man on the hill
To keep watch, while they all rode onward,
Into the Valley of Death until they stood
Under the boughs heavily laden with fruit,
Which gave the appearance of golden pears.

Without delay, King Frederic took off his
Coat and then removed from around his arm
Old bandages thick with putrid puss. They
Were immediately filled with concern, for
Gangrene had turned his flesh solid black,
And if left untreated would soon kill him.
Everywhere was the sweet fragrance of God.
So Major Reynolds plucked some fruit from
A low bough, and gave it to King Frederic,
And said, "Eat," and so he ate about half,
Then spread what was left of the fruit on
His wound which healed somehow, instantly.

When the others saw how King Frederic had
Groaned in ecstasy, they wanted to eat of
The fruit that tastes like honey; but, as
Soon as they ate, they felt those effects
Which turn men mad, because on Earth they
Desired treasure belonging only to Heaven.
Suddenly, their five senses, taste, touch,
Sound, smell, and sight became a lot more
Sensitive. Soon they heard doves singing
Songs high up in the boughs, and the loud
Trumpet of horns and harps, on the breeze,
Accompanied by a glorious choir of Angels.

At that moment, the rider who watched for
The enemy, spurred his horse down hill at
Breakneck speed, now slipping and sliding,
Until he quickly reined in his horse next
To the trunk of the Tree, where they were
Busily dreaming dreams and seeing visions.
"Major Reynolds, I have spotted the enemy.
We must leave!" the young Lieutenant said,
Speaking very loud so they could hear him.
Right then, Major Reynolds frightened the
Lieutenant by telling him what the others
Had implicitly come to understand already.

"We stay while King Frederic escapes harm."
Seeing much fear in the Lieutenant's eyes,
Major Reynolds gave him of the fruit, and
Then said, "Eat," and from that moment on
He felt at peace, and said, "I understand,
God shall grant us eternal life in Heaven."
Suddenly, they heard a thunderous beating
Of horses' hooves from the oncoming enemy,
So many, the birds flew from the branches.
Major Reynolds then said to King Frederic,
"Make haste sire, for there's little time.
Soon, giant waves shall come and drown us."

So, King Frederic paused just long enough
To fill his saddlebags with lots of fruit,
Before turning to salute all his officers,
Who made ready for the ultimate sacrifice.
Meanwhile King Frederic rode Absalom from
The valley, and stopped on the next ridge.
From there, King Frederic eagerly watched,
While his men shot their arrows from bows,
Killing dozens of Pazmanians. Only after,
After the last brave hero had fallen like
Ripe fruit did King Frederic spur Absalom,
Then gallop away, his eyes wet with tears.

Hardly more than an hour had passed, when
Edmund came on the scene, in the hopes of
Finding in the dead that were lying about
In the meadows, the body of King Frederic,
Who he wished to identify, so there could
Be no doubt at all that Frederic was dead.
But when he asked General Rudolph to show
Him where his body fell among the corpses,
Edmund was in for a big surprise, when he
Heard General Rudolph reply, "I've had my
Men look everywhere, sire, but the King's
Nowhere to be found throughout the valley."

Just then, Edmund's volcanic fury erupted,
On a level General Rudolph had never seen
Before now, when he said, shouting loudly,
While running here, there, and everywhere
Looking at each face, hoping to recognize
His handsome older brother, King Frederic,
"I ask you to do this thing, and you fail!
I'm forever cursed by fools and imbeciles.
All of my officers are either corrupt and
Incompetent, or too incompetent to become
Corrupt; how can I ever rule this country
When all the people in it are nincompoops?"

Just then, General Rudolph was rescued by
None other than Ambassador Bourbon, whose
Suave and sophisticated diplomacy preened
Edmund's hurt ruffled feathers, by saying,
"Calm down, Edmund; I shall persuade King
Hooligan to loan you the black Dragon who
Can sniff out King Frederic's whereabouts,
Doing this more quickly than even a hound.
We only need something King Frederic wore."
Suddenly, Edmund found the coat that King
Frederic had lost in haste, and then said,
"My brother's coat, give it to the Dragon."

BOOK TWO

When King Frederic woke up and then found
He was lying in a strange bed, in an even
Stranger room with a crucifix on the wall,
He grew frantic to remember what happened,
Because his memories of recent events had
Been wiped clean like a school chalkboard.
Right then, he stared at the monk who had
Introduced himself as Father Saint Pierre,
The tenth Monsignor at the Abbey of Trent.
Suddenly, he felt hollow as if hot embers
Burned a hole in his soul, and then asked,
"How long have I stayed here at the Abbey?"

"All of two weeks," Monsignor Pierre said,
In a calm, reassuring, intelligent manner.
"Ever since Miguel, our shepherd boy went
To the stream to water his flock of sheep,
As he does each morning, except on Sunday,
And then discovered you lying unconscious.
Do you recall how you got that neck wound?"
"No, I've tried to remember what happened.
But my mind has lost memory of this event,"
King Frederic said. Now Monsignor Pierre
Walked over to go out the door. "You may
Have amnesia and need only rest," he said.

When the monk had gone, King Frederic was
Determined to remember something, even if
It made no sense, and so he shut his eyes,
And relaxed, and then concentrated on the
First memory to float up in his conscious.
For a long time King Frederic saw nothing.
Then, all at once, some memories appeared,
First, confused images, then whole scenes,
Which showed him being struck from behind,
Being knocked from his horse by something,
And then looking up in the sky, he saw it,
The black Dragon, returning for him again.

King Frederic then sat bolt upright in bed,
His eyes opened, and focused on the window,
After having seen something that terrified
Him, something that his conscious mind had
Tried hard to suppress until now, when the
Event tumbled from his memory like a flood.
It was then he realized that sweat covered
His body and that his hand shook from fear.
Soon, he lay back down on the mattress and
Closed his eyes, and that's when he saw it
Again, and he was transported back in time
To when he was running, after being struck

From behind by a monster, the black Dragon,
Whose bat like wings turned in the air, on
The instant, and then swiftly came for him.
Frantically, he searched for some place to
Hide, when he saw a cave with a small neck
Like a bottle and then squeezed through it.
Once inside of the cave, he found he could
Stand up straight without hitting his head,
And that he could feel along the wall with
His hands, until he reached the spot where
He no longer heard the black Dragon, still
Roaring with blind tyrannical rage outside.

Suddenly, he paused to touch his sore neck,
And for the first time, he felt blood, and
He became dizzy, and vomited on the ground,
Just as if his nerves had reacted to venom.
Afterward he felt weak and lay in the cave,
Until the break of day, when he remembered
Glancing up, and seeing a beam of sunlight
Pouring down through a hole in the ceiling,
And he remembered climbing up on the rocks,
And walking down a road, until he lay down
To drink water from a cold mountain stream,
Then nothing, as his mind went blank again.

King Frederic heard Gregorian chants being
Sung by a choir of monks, somewhere inside
Of the monastery. This choir of all males
Had soothing voices, and intrigued him, so
He got dressed and then followed the sound
Down the hall, until he came to the chapel.
Inside of the chapel, a Priest was hearing
Confessions; without understanding why, he
Felt compelled to go in the booth and then
Kneel by the window, through whose diamond
Shaped wooden lattice he could clearly see,
In the darkness, the Priest's covered head.

But immediately, King Frederic believed he
Had made a mistake by going there, because
He felt shy and awkward about telling this
Total stranger his inmost private thoughts.
Sensing this was the case, the Priest said,
"You can't shock me; I've heard everything."
So, King Frederic told him a story, saying,
"I died, then I woke up in a strange place,
With three murderous men, whom I could not
See on account of it was pitch black there.
When I reflected on where I was, the first
Heard my thoughts, somehow, for he said to

To me in a sudden burst of anger, "Shut up!"
Then I heard a second man nearby, who said,
"You are in Hell!" I felt disoriented and
Confused because they had read my thoughts.
Suddenly, when I heard a third man mock me,
Saying, "Yes sire, and you belong here too!"
I hoped they were wrong, but the heat that
I felt was unbearable. It made me thirsty.
But there wasn't a drop of water, anywhere."
Suddenly, King Frederic felt too exhausted
To continue his story; thanking the Priest
Who prayed for him, he soon left the booth.

Right after eating supper in the cafeteria
With the monks, King Frederic came back to
His room, where he immediately lay down on
The bed with a headache. When closing his
Eyes, hundreds of terrifying memories soon
Flooded his mind, until he woke up, afraid.
King Frederic felt he had been in darkness
With the ruler of the underworld, that one
The world knows by the name Satan or Devil.
He had seen him sitting high upon a throne,
Holding a three pronged triton in one hand,
And in the other hand, a long slender whip.

Satan was the color of dried blood, a dark
Red, and there were a pair of curved horns
Upon his head, like those of a ram or goat.
All around, people were screaming in agony
As they rushed over to him, and then asked
For a drop of water to quench their thirst.
When King Frederic said he had no water to
Give them, they didn't believe him and got
Very angry; some mocked him and cursed him,
And some punched him and kicked him, still
Others bit him and would grind their teeth,
Until it seemed a mob might tear him apart.

Though the people numbered in the millions,
King Frederic fought back with great vigor,
Boxing them or kicking them, until he grew
Full of rage and he began to swear in vain.
It was then he noticed they hesitated when
He spoke the name Jesus, which he repeated
Over and over again until they were silent,
And losing interest, they started to drift
Away. Soon, King Frederic sank and lay on
The floor, his spirit body feeling so weak,
He believed right at that moment, he might
Boil, diffuse, and then vanish in thin air.

Several days later, King Frederic returned
To the booth that had the same Priest, who
Had already heard his previous confessions,
And he said, "I had another nightmare, and
Now I can remember more details about what
Happened in the time that I burned in Hell."
So the Priest reached a hand in the pocket
Of his brown robe and removed prayer beads.
"I believe you had a near-death-experience,"
The Priest went on, "tell me what happened."
King Frederic paused for a moment to clear
Out the mucus from his throat, and he said,

"The last thing I told you was that I went
To Hell, because I felt separated from God.
But what I didn't tell you was this, I had
Learned much later, that my mother heard a
Voice from Heaven, telling her, pray, your
Son is dying. Being a very good Christian,
My mother prayed, and right at that moment,
I could read her words, written on papyrus,
In what appeared to be a scriptural scroll.
Then suddenly, I saw a bright light appear,
Just a small speck shining in the distance.
But soon it grew big, then hovered over me.

Then suddenly, I got sucked up into a void,
A huge vortex the size of a tornado, and I
Flew along the tunnel at unheard of speeds.
I saw a bright light at the other end, and
Standing within it there was the figure of
A man, who could only be our savior, Jesus.
As I got closer, this magnificent being of
Light began to pulsate in rhythmical waves.
As the first wave passed through my spirit,
All of a sudden, I felt unconditional love.
When the second wave hit me, a few seconds
Later, I felt an overwhelming sense of joy."

At this point in his story, King Frederic
Paused, as if overcome by strong emotions
That caused tears to roll down his cheeks.
Choked up, he couldn't speak again, until
A few seconds had passed, when he went on
To tell the Priest, "But I have bored you!
Perhaps I should be quiet, I should leave."
But the Priest insisted he stay, and said,
"No sire, please don't stop on my account.
You know how to tell a good story, and by
Keeping it interesting, I hope you finish."
Encouraged by this, King Frederic went on.

"When I grew bolder being in his presence,
I asked Jesus if I could come even closer.
I wanted to see his face through the veil
Of clouds that swirled with bright colors,
Many of them unknown, never seen on earth.
To my surprise, Jesus replied, "Come here."
"Soon as I came through the bright clouds,
I could see the nail marks from the cross,
Which sadly disfigured his hands and feet.
He had on sandals, plus a white robe with
A gold sash around his waist; neither one
Was made from cloth, but from woven light.

However, much as I wanted to see his face,
I felt blinded by light of a billion suns.
When we spoke, we did not use our tongues,
And yet our thoughts were heard, unspoken,
By a conveyance, something like telepathy.
When he saw that I was coming even closer,
Jesus suddenly stepped aside, pointing to
That other end of the tunnel, where I saw
Birds, trees, rivers, and fields, feeling
All joyous in the spirit of the Lord, God.
Then I felt afraid because Jesus asked me,
"Do you deserve eternal life, in Paradise?"

"I felt crushed. I knew I didn't deserve
Heaven, for Hell is the place for sinners.
When I asked the Lord how to reach Heaven,
He simply said, "Believe in me and in the
One who sent me." Then I returned, so my
Mother would not believe I died a heathen."
It was late when confession was over, and
So King Frederic went back to his room to
Read a book, before falling asleep in bed.
Then the very next morning, King Frederic
Woke up and looked out at the pink clouds,
As if seeing a sunrise for the first time.

Feeling that if he stayed in bed a second
Longer he might burst from pent up energy,
King Frederic dressed in borrowed clothes
And then went outside, to walk around the
Monastery grounds in the cool air of dawn.
It was this time of day he liked the best.
No one stirred at this hour, not even the
Monks who rushed to early morning prayers.
All the more reason why King Frederic was
Surprised to see the shepherd boy, Miguel,
Who had found him half dead at the stream,
Now opening the gate to let out the sheep.

When Miguel said he was leading his flock
On their annual trek up the mountain side
So they could feed on the summer pastures,
King Frederic asked, "May I come with you?"
So Miguel said, "If you do, I'll show you
The hidden caves where the Togalons lived."
King Frederic was curious about the caves
Inhabited by the Togalons, who, according
To legend, and recent findings discovered
From archeology, were an advanced race of
People who thrived at a time of civil war,
And for some reason, suddenly disappeared.

So King Frederic and Miguel began to climb
Up the trail, on the mountain's north face.
Two hours later, they came to an odd place
Where they saw a series of small caves dug
High up in the rock cliffs. King Frederic
Said to Miguel, "Have you tried to explore
Any of those caves up at the top?" Miguel
Shook his head, saying, "No, it's bad luck.
Some monks say all of the caves are cursed."
Yet King Frederic wanted to look inside of
The caves, and went up the cliff alone, as
Miguel remained below to play on his flute.

But the caves were empty and King Frederic
Started to climb back down the cliff again.
It was then that Miguel said, "Let me play
You the only old Togalon song I know about."
As Miguel blew a series of notes, suddenly,
A rock slid back to reveal a cave entrance.
As King Frederic started to enter the cave,
Miguel shouted, saying, "Don't go in there!
The ghosts will haunt your dreams at night!"
But King Frederic went in the cave, anyway.
Inside, it was dark, the air smelled musty.
Then suddenly, a room blazed with sunlight.

Looking on in amazement, King Frederic saw
The man's full skeleton, yellowed with age,
Sitting at a table with his head bent over
A book, penned in the old Togalon language.
A sword bedecked with jewels hung from his
Waist, still sheathed in a gilded scabbard.
Removing the book that lay under his skull,
King Frederic blew off layers of fine dust,
Before he retrieved the sword and scabbard,
Then walked outside to meet up with Miguel,
Who shut the door again, by playing on his
Flute the very same notes, only in reverse.

Later that afternoon, when they descended
The mountainside, driving the flock along
The same meandering pathway they had come,
King Frederic let Miguel open up the gate
To put sheep in a corral, behind the barn,
While he went to the library in the Abbey.
Here King Frederic found Monsignor Pierre,
A scholar of Latin, and ancient languages,
Who slowly perused a few pages, then said,
"This book is a diary, written in Togalon,
By a man whose name was Tarsus. You have
Made an important discovery." So he read

One section, and said, "My name is Tarsus,
The last survivor of a proud noble family.
As I write this, all of my three children
Are deceased from laboratory disease that
All but exterminated a nation of Togalons.
Recently I have come from burying my wife,
Acacia, in a grave with our dear children,
Who rest under pine trees along the slope.
We Togalons grievously erred when we made
The black Dragon, capable of germ warfare,
The most dreaded weapon in our civil wars.
True, we did forge a sword with the power

To slay the black Dragon, but I could not
Let my poor family go hungry without food,
So I pried the ruby from the sword's hilt,
Then sold the gem to a wandering merchant
From the distant, fertile land of Alettas,
For less than a bushel of rotten potatoes.
We were starving; what choices did I have?
The sword grew powerless without its ruby
To defeat the Dragon and now all are dead.
Even now, as I write this, my hand shakes
From palsy. Soon, I will perish and then
Haunt these caves with other uneasy souls."

Suddenly, King Frederic told the Monsignor
How he had found the sword inside the cave,
Strapped around the wasted bones of Tarsus,
And that the sword was located in his room.
Without delay, Monsignor Pierre went along
With King Frederic, who went in his closet
And then came out with the Sword of Tarsus,
Which Monsignor Pierre examined, in minute
Detail, before answering, "There were only
Twelve of these swords made by Theophanous,
The master artisan, who forged them in the
Fiery volcano of Tephra, during the golden

Age of Togalon. All of them were supposed
To have been destroyed by the Oracles long
Ago, when they were plunged in an acid vat,
At the same time the black Dragon vanished.
The sword is missing a ruby, which gave it
Power, but still has three precious stones:
Pink diamond, green emerald, blue sapphire,
Which gave the sword selective versatility."
King Frederic thought in silence, and said,
"I will travel to Alettas to find the ruby.
If the Oracles made the black Dragon, they
Also made the sword as a way to destroy it."

"Centuries have passed, since Tarsus wrote
His story in the cave. You may be wasting
Your time," Monsignor Pierre said, at last.
"But what choice do I have?" King Frederic
Said. "If I don't find the ruby, everyone
Here will die from the black Dragon's bite.
I will leave for Drake's Bay tomorrow, and
Then find a ship that is bound for Alettas."
"Then take this," Monsignor Pierre replied,
Giving him a coin purse. "I may give alms,
From charity, to humble and poor travelers."
In this way King Frederic was blest by God.

Frederic waited just a week in Drake's Bay
Before he got on board a small sturdy ship,
Called the Albatross, which, being a sloop,
Had two tall masts, with broad white sails
Billowing in the wind, above the bow waves,
When setting out for the shores of Alettas.
Quickly the ship sailed, on wings unfurled,
Like the sea-going bird that bore its name,
That could be seen soaring high in the sky,
At times, hundreds of miles away from land,
A lone brave heart that endured all storms,
And spells of calm even, to reach its home.

When three weeks out at sea, the Albatross
Ran into a storm with hurricane winds that
Drove the ship into rough tumultuous waves,
Which rocked the bow and stern, to and fro,
So hard all of the passengers and crew now
Believed they would sink many fathoms deep.
But fortunately, they sailed under a stout
Captain, James Thaddeus Cobb, who knew how
To navigate through these uncharted waters,
Having traded in seaports around the world.
Although many of the men on board the ship
Were afraid of their Captain, they trusted

His astute mariner's knowledge of the seas.
All at once, they leaped at his command to
Turn the ship away from Alettas, and point
It in the direction of Rangoon Island, and
The small harbor, whose serrated mountains
Would protect them from the dangerous gale.
Then everyone's heart was filled with hope,
Believing they would soon reach the harbor.
But, what not even a seasoned sailor could
Have known is that, instead of moving away,
They headed directly into the storm itself,
Its southern winds blowing twice as strong.

Now, on continuous watch, the men slept in
Their clothes, which were soaking wet from
Battling big waves that washed on the deck.
Working in shifts like a fire brigade, men
Bailed out the bilge using leather buckets,
Passing them down the line to the next man.
Right then, when the Albatross seemed like
It would founder from some gargantuan wave,
Captain Cobb ordered his crew to throw all
Of the heavy cargo they had over the sides.
This they did in great haste to get rid of
Large wooden crates filled with porcelains

And perfumes, silver plates and silk gowns,
Sawn lumber, plus barrels of wine and fish.
Soon one sailor, suddenly washed overboard,
Was seen floating in the ship's foamy wake.
In the hope no more of the men would drown,
Each one tied a long rope around his waist.
When new waves set the timbers a shivering,
Captain Cobb lamented the loss of the ship,
This until the watchman in the crow's nest,
High at the top of the mast, began to yell
Words that warmed the cockles of his heart,
Saying, "Land ahoy! Off the starboard bow!"

Quickly looking westward, over the horizon,
Captain Cobb could see the island shrouded
In fog. Shouting to the helmsman, he said,
"Steer a course for Rangoon! The Lord has
Held back his great wrath from love of his
People, and shall soon bring all to safety."
Once the crew had climbed the ropes of the
Masts and lowered the sails, the Albatross
Spread its wings and flew inside the small
Harbor, where iron anchors were dropped on
The leeward side, near the towering cliffs,
And for three days they rode out the storm.

Later, in the quiet aftermath of the storm,
When Captain Cobb had ordered an inventory
Of the ship's larder, it was discovered to
The crew's surprise that many wood barrels
With salted meat were jettisoned overboard
By accident, when easing the heavy ballast.
Fearing they will soon run out of victuals,
During that voyage to Alettas, still ahead,
Captain Cobb gave the order to cut rations
By as much as two thirds. Naturally, this
Caused discontent among all of the sailors,
Who opened kegs of rum, without permission.

When inebriated, they held talks of mutiny
That were led by a gruff red haired sailor,
Known to everyone there simply by the name
Of Big Red, who shouted, saying, "I'll not
Sail with Captain Cobb, who is a damn fool.
I didn't sign on to slowly starve to death.
A reasonable man will turn the ship around
And then go back to port for more supplies.
I'm not afraid to take control of the helm.
Who here has guts to help me take the ship?"
Although a majority wanted to mutiny, some
Were afraid, and said, "How shall we do it?"

So Big Red told them of his plan, and said,
"You all know a passenger onboard the ship
Is Leilani, the Princess of Alettas. With
Her as our hostage, our treasure, our hope,
Captain Cobb will have no choice, but turn
This ship, and head straight back to Arden."
"I'll join you," one sailor said. "Me too,"
A second said. In all, four sailors vowed
To help Big Red, who toasted their success,
Before he took notice of a stranger, known
To them only as Frederic, who had traveled
Incognito by keeping his identity a secret.

All of a sudden, Big Red became suspicious
Of Frederic, as he lay on his bunk, inside
Of the forecastle, pretending to be asleep.
Jumping to his feet, he got a lantern from
The overhead beam, and then swaggered over
To talk with Frederic, who turned his head
To meet Big Red's challenging stare, while
Shielding his eyes from the bright lantern.
"Want a drink?" Big Red asked, now holding
A clay jug of molasses rum in front of him.
When Frederic shook his head and said, "No,"
Big Red instantly looked at his companions,

And said, "This sure is one curious fellow.
He's silent as a mouse, he stays all alone,
And he turns down my friendly drink of rum."
Suddenly, a drunken sailor joked, and said,
"Maybe he misses home, and his dear mother,"
Bringing quick laughter from the other men.
Big Red resumed speaking, "Here's the poop.
Me and the boys are tired of short rations.
We plan to highjack this ship from Captain
Cobb and his officers, then turn it around
And head back to Arden, where we first met
Captain Cobb and agreed to hire on as crew.

We wants to know, will you join up with us?"
Frederic knew the consequences if he dared
To refuse, but he voted with his conscious,
And said, "I won't be a part of any mutiny."
Feeling angry, Big Red said, "Have it your
Way, friend. But don't you try to stop us.
If you do, I'll kill you myself." And Big
Red slowly drew a finger across his throat.
Then all of the sailors climbed the ladder
And went topside, where they began to work,
As though this day would be like any other,
When knowing it would be anything but that.

By the third week at sea, everyone onboard
The ship had established a kind of routine.
It was no less true for two very important
People, namely Princess Leilani of Alettas,
That vivacious twenty year old daughter of
King Alto, plus her Governess, Marsha Moss.
Each morning, after having eaten breakfast
In the cabin, these guests of Captain Cobb,
These fair young maidens, would take their
Exercise by walking around the ship's deck,
When they talked about all sorts of things,
While taking in the sunshine and fresh air.

But the different thing about this morning
Was that they were met at the storage room
By Big Red and the other four sailors, who
Had waited in hiding, until they were near,
Then jumped out to abduct Princess Leilani,
By pulling a burlap bag down over her head.
When three of the men started to run after
The Governess, Big Red yelled loud, saying,
"Let her go, boys! We got our ticket home!
Now everyone jump into the hold, using the
Rungs of the ladder; be quick about it too,
So I can pass down my lively little bundle."

Right after they had tied Princess Leilani
To the largest mast using woven hemp ropes,
Big Red wrote a note to Captain Cobb, with
These words, "Turn the ship around Captain,
Or else a Princess's blood be on your head."
Then he had Ripcan take it to Captain Cobb,
Who read the note, quickly arrested Ripcan,
Charged him with abduction and mutiny, and
Hastened to unlock the armory in his cabin,
Where he supplied his officers with swords,
Saying, "As long as I live and breathe air,
You will follow the orders of your Captain."

When everything was prepared, Captain Cobb
Yelled down in the hold, telling them what
To do, "Send her up the ladder!" he roared.
"Then climb up, with hands over your heads!"
However, Big Red only repeated his demands,
"Turn the ship around, or we kill the girl!"
Suddenly, Captain Cobb's voice quivered in
Anger, as he made one last attempt, saying,
"If you let the girl go, and you surrender,
I promise to reduce the number of lashings.
Harm her, and you shall hang from the mast!"
Everyone knew he had meant every word, too.

But still, the mutineers refused to listen.
They broke open the boxes of rationed food,
Then tapped the barrels of rum, eating and
And drinking, until their stomachs were no
Longer hungry but satisfied, while waiting
For Captain Cobb to relinquish his command.
Meanwhile, Frederic bided his time, waited
For the moment when he could free Princess
Leilani, who was a hostage at the mercy of
Those villainous men, who had already made
Threats on her life, and would do anything,
It seemed, to turn the ship homeward bound.

It came at around twelve o'clock, midnight,
When all the sailors were drunk, and sound
Asleep in the bunk beds, including the man
Who was supposed to keep watch on Princess
Leilani, who now had to sleep slumped over,
Because her ropes were tied to a main mast.
Frederic waited on his bunk with both eyes
Closed, until the others had fallen asleep.
Then he crept forward on his tip toes, and
Freed Princess Leilani by cutting the rope
With a knife. Instantly, Princess Leilani
Sprang to her feet and raced up the ladder.

Then Frederic climbed up the ladder, still
Unaware of what waited for him on the deck,
Until they surrounded him, all of a sudden,
Several officers with swords, and he heard
A voice, Captain Cobb's shout, "Arrest him!
He is just as guilty as the other brigands!"
Feeling stricken by the conduct of Captain
Cobb, Princess Leilani complained bitterly,
Saying, "He freed me from my abductors and
Should be released." However, Marsha Moss
Realized Captain Cobb hated to take orders
From a woman, so she took Princess Leilani

By the hand, and walked her to their cabin.
Meanwhile, Captain Cobb went down a ladder
Ahead of his officers, into the cargo hold,
Where all of the sailors, drunk and asleep,
Woke up all of a sudden, only to find that
Everyone had been chained in iron shackles.
Later, at the first crack of morning light,
Captain Cobb ordered his officers to rouse
Those men from slumbers, in which they had
Nightmares, they knew had come true, while
They stood sober at the mast, with a noose
Around their necks, all ready to be hanged.

To his surprise, Frederic stood among them.
"Do you have anything more you wish to say?"
Captain Cobb whined in a high shrill voice,
"Before I sentence you together for crimes
Punishable by death?" Big Red sobbed, "We
Was starving; we'd never hurt the Princess."
But, Captain Cobb had no mercy in his cold
Dead eyes, as he raised his arm in the air,
Ready to give a signal that they be hanged.
Then suddenly it happened, Count Darby had
Recognized King Frederic, and then said to
Captain Cobb, "Wait! Let this prisoner go!"

This was because Count Darby knew Frederic
And Edmund, having gone to the same school,
He being part of the same privileged class
Of noble Ardenians, who had remained loyal
To King Edmund, who would enrich his lands
And pay a big reward for Frederic's return.
So Count Darby bargained with Captain Cobb,
By promising one half of this reward money
In exchange for making Frederic a prisoner,
A better deal than Cobb gave the mutineers,
Whose punishment for their crime was to be
Hanged by the neck, until dead, dead, dead.

Soon after this punishment was carried out,
The Albatross departed from Rangoon Island
For those distant fertile lands of Alettas,
To which they came, after three more weeks,
Sailing with fair weather and steady winds.
Here, a curious crowd met them at the dock,
That same forenoon, where Princess Leilani
Watched in sorrow, as they hauled Frederic
In a wagon, bound for the county jailhouse.
Then, Princess Leilani went ashore, in the
Company of her Governess, Marsha Moss, who
Helped her search for her father King Alto,

Who waited to pick them up in his carriage.
When King Alto's one and only heir greeted
Her father with affection, and immediately
Told him that the former King of Arden had
Rescued her, from five men who mutinied on
The ship, but is now being held a prisoner,
King Alto knew he had to do something, and
Said, "I shall help Frederic, since Harold,
His father, who was my benefactor long ago,
Chose him as his heir, and not his brother,
Edmund, who usurped both crown and kingdom."
"Please do, father," Princess Leilani said.

Then later on, at ten o'clock that evening,
Just as the old jailor sat down at a table
To eat his cold porridge, he heard a quick
Rap on the iron knocker, by someone at the
Door. Feeling mad, he limped over to open
Up the latch, and then peered out, talking,
"I got no time to eats my victuals tonight.
Who comes a calling me at such a late hour?
Perhaps thieves who would cudgel my brains,
If I were dumb, and I let them come inside.
Now I ask ye, give your names, and show me
Your faces within the bright lantern light?"

"This is Colonel Drayton, Commander of the
Royal Guards," a gruff voice shouted, from
Without; "Hurry up, you old goat, before I
Make you sweep out the barn until doomsday!"
"Now there's no need to insult me, Colonel.
Kindness is best," that old jailor scolded.
Just then, when the heavy iron barred door
Swung open, Colonel Drayton stepped across
The entrance, with a young Lieutenant, who
Soon revealed an official looking document,
Signed with King Alto's authentic wax seal.
"Bring Frederic," Colonel Drayton demanded.

Squinting up his eyes, the old jailor read
Several paragraphs through wire spectacles.
He then shrugged and shuffled off to bring
Frederic, who was eager to leave that jail,
But refused to go, unless he was given all
Of his things, including his sack of fruit
From the Tree of Life, and his weapon, the
Sword of Tarsus, which the old jailor took
Down from a closet, and handed to Frederic,
Saying, "And what shall I tell Count Darby?"
Believing this old jailor a fool, Frederic
Responded, "Tell Count Darby to go to Hell!"

Outside, in the pouring rain, Frederic saw
A large carriage, and a team of six horses,
Parked at the curb, by the brick jailhouse.
When the Lieutenant held open the door and
He had climbed in on the seat, he felt the
Jolt of the carriage as the horses started
On the road, paved with rough cobblestones.
While many questions needed to be answered,
Frederic stayed calm and reflected on what
Colonel Drayton had told him earlier, that
He would become the guest of King Alto and
Princess Leilani, who waited at the palace.

About one hour later, when Frederic yelled
Through the window at Colonel Drayton, and
Then said, "When shall we reach the palace?"
That officer said, hunched inside a poncho,
In the driving rain, "Soon I reckon, since
The river has ceased to overflow its banks."
After ten minutes, the carriage entered in
Through a gate, watched over by two marble
Lions, on either side of a curved driveway,
Before coming to a halt at the front steps
Of the royal palace, where a white servant,
Who wore a black tuxedo, welcomed Frederic,

Saying, "King Alto is not here to meet you.
He goes to bed at the same time each night,
At nine o'clock. But he expects you to be
On the porch for breakfast, at six o'clock."
"I will be there of course," Frederic said,
And he followed the servant into the lobby.
It was here that Frederic saw a display of
Ancestral crowns and felt a tugging on the
Sword of Tarsus as one golden crown topped
With a rare precious ruby suddenly slammed
Hard against the glass of the display case
And started to vibrate, chattering noisily.

Frederic felt stunned, the Sword of Tarsus
Had found the ruby almost immediately, and
Even now when he turned away to follow the
White servant up the long marble staircase,
Frederic could feel it tugging at the ruby,
With an irresistible invisible force still,
As he went down the length of the corridor,
It only stopping when the servant unlocked
The door with a metal key and then went in
The chamber to illume a crystal chandelier,
By lighting dozens of candles with a flame,
And Frederic had shut the door behind them.

The white servant piled logs on the hearth
To be rid of a damp musty chill in the air,
And quickly had a warm blaze burning there.
"King Alto expects all of his guests to be
On time for breakfast," the pale faced man
Said, "Consequently, I'll wake you at five."
Frederic felt tired and was glad the white
Servant had gone. The moment Frederic lay
Under the covers with his head on a pillow,
He drifted off to sleep, listening to rain
Falling on the window as lightning flashed
And thunder rumbled over the distant hills.

Then at five, the white servant knocked on
The door, and woke Frederic up, as planned.
After pouring hot water into the metal tub,
The white servant left Frederic, all alone,
So he could bathe right inside the privacy
Of his bedroom, where a fireplace crackled.
When Frederic dried off with a thick towel,
He noticed that the white servant had laid
Clean fresh clothes on the back of a chair,
Taken from King Alto's wardrobe, and so he
Got dressed, and then left him a small tip,
And then went downstairs to meet his hosts.

However, when Frederic went onto the porch
To meet King Alto, and the two ladies, the
Princess Leilani and her Governess, Marsha
Moss, he was surprised to meet Count Darby,
Who drew a sword on the instant he saw him,
And said as a warning to King Alto, saying,
"How dare you hide this man in your palace?
I insist that you arrest this criminal and
Then turn him over to me so I can take him
Back to Arden, where he'll be tried before
King Edmund, who may consider your actions
A declaration of war if you fail to comply."

Now Frederic wished he had taken the Sword
Of Tarsus from the bedroom closet where he
Had it stored. But fortunately, King Alto
Felt offended by Count Darby and asked him
To leave, saying, "You're not welcome here.
Depart Alettas, or my men shall arrest you!"
This made Count Darby angry, and he made a
Second threat, this time aimed at Frederic,
When he said, "Our paths shall cross again,
At a time more advantageous than right now.
Then I will teach you a lesson in humility,
By seeing you apprehended and horsewhipped."

There were three more gentlemen with Count
Darby, and they all soon departed inside a
Big covered carriage, drawn by four horses.
When they had gone, King Alto stood up and
Then said, "But I forget my manners. Take
No heed of those four dislikeable villains."
Now to Frederic, "Share in our hospitality,
And eat of the good food for which Alettas
Is famous. Here we men like to boast that
We possess the most beautiful women in the
World, of which these two ladies are proof.
My boy you could do far worse than Alettas."

Soon, laughter was heard from the Princess,
Who poked fun at King Alto, when saying to
Frederic, "Never mind my father's comments.
He wants me to accept the first suitor who
Shows at court with a willingness to marry
So he can love and spoil his grandchildren."
King Alto took exception to this, and said,
"You should be a mother, and I should be a
Grandfather; the country needs a male heir."
"And it shall have one, only not right now,"
Princess Leilani said, "like most women of
Today, I'll wait before I have my children."

But King Alto didn't want her to wait, and
Said, "But I grow old, I have frosty hairs.
I would teach the young prince how to hunt,
And all manly things; he must know when to
Use the art of diplomacy and the skills of
War, and how to reside over our parliament."
But Princess Leilani refused to budge, and
Said, "What if they are all girls, no boys?
Would you have girls command your officers
In a cavalry charge? Or would girls fight
Against men who swing swords during battle?
I think the weaker sex will become worsted."

Now King Alto knew when he had been beaten,
And said, "O how my heart pounds like iron
Between the hammer and anvil. You can not
Find a King more sad than me if you looked
Round the whole world! You conquer reason
With love, and yet defeat love with reason.
I'm glad my wife, Etta, God bless her soul,
Is not here to see my sad state of affairs.
She would not approve of this modern world.
I can't take on a new wife to bear me more
Children; old trees bear little good fruit.
Now stop it; I fear that we bore our guest."

But, Frederic didn't feel bored. He liked
To hear them talk around a breakfast table,
Like any other family in Alettas. Yet, he
Was glad too King Alto made the suggestion
That they change the topic of conversation.
Eager to oblige him, Princess Leilani said,
"After the rain last night, the morning is
Washed and cleaned. Look, the sun appears
Like a golden discus hurled by a Greek god.
It's a perfect day for horseback riding in
The country. Frederic, Marsha and I would
Feel honored to include you in our company."

"But, I don't have a horse," Frederic said.
"Well, I'm sure my father can lend you one,"
Princess Leilani said, "he has dozens; you
May pick your horse from any in the stable."
"Yes," King Alto said, "except for the bay,
With Arab blood, which no one rides but me."
So it was settled. While Princess Leilani
And Marsha Moss went to change into riding
Clothes, Frederic stayed behind, and spoke
With King Alto, saying, "Sir, you have put
All Alettas at risk by refusing to turn me
Over to Count Darby. I'd like to know why

You want to protect a complete stranger in
Your kingdom?" To which King Alto replied,
"This is easy; your father King Harold and
I fought at each other's side at the First
Lutheran War, against the Pazmania scourge.
I feel obligated to protect his eldest son."
Suddenly they were interrupted by Princess
Leilani, who said to her father, "Will you
Come with us, daddy?" But, King Alto said,
"Perhaps tomorrow, dear; age has undone me."
Ignoring Leilani, King Alto became lost in
Reverie, remembering the days of his youth.

Once at the stables, Frederic picked out a
Large black stallion whose lineage all but
Guaranteed a brave spirit, whose speed and
Strength surpassed both mares, all enjoyed
During their ride out in the country today.
Frederic didn't mind their constant escort.
But after a while Frederic felt encumbered,
Since Princess Leilani invariably traveled
With this band of four guards, who closely
Trailed behind them, ready to help her out
In any emergency, if the need should arise.
Princess Leilani felt exactly the same way.

Just before this, she had arranged to lose
These four guards, by enlisting the aid of
Marsha Moss, who would distract them, just
Long enough so that she and Frederic could
Race on ahead, spurring both horses, until
They disappeared around a bend in the road.
At once, the four guards chased after them,
Riding in hot pursuit. But, the Governess,
Marsha Moss, deceived the guards once more
By leading them passed a grove of hemlocks,
In which Princess Leilani and Frederic hid,
Amused at watching everyone go right on by.

Afterward, after the four guards were gone,
Princess Leilani led the way there, taking
A short cut through a primeval rain forest,
Whose limpid water flowed down in cascades
Before meandering around the river's banks,
Where they both stopped to rest the horses.
Then Princess Leilani, feeling inspired by
Their recent prank, took off her shoes and
Bathed her feet in a mirrored pool, before
She dropped in Frederic's mouth with juice
Stained finger and thumb a wild strawberry,
So Frederic may taste the sweets in nature.

Then Princess Leilani took Frederic's hand,
Held it within her hand, and peered within
His blue eyes to see if they sparkled with
Desire. Believing they did, she tilted up
Her head, and kissed his lips with passion.
But soon, she separated from him, and said,
"Maybe my father was right, I should marry,
And make him happy, by giving him children
To play around his feet; yet, I think good
Husbands are hard to find, today. Perhaps
I should marry you, because my suitors who
Would woo me at court dances leave me cold."

Feeling amazed, Frederic said, "Do all the
Women of Alettas speak to men as boldly as
The Princess?" Just then Princess Leilani
Smiled, then said, "We are taught to speak
Our minds at a tender age. Would you like
A bold wife? Many men are put off by them."
"You should have asked me before we kissed,"
Frederic said, "I am a happily married man."
Suddenly, something happened that Frederic
Didn't understand, at first. The Princess
Pushed him violently to one side, and then
Moved in front to shield him with her body.

Now Frederic learned why, when an assassin,
Hidden by a clump of trees, shot his arrow
And wounded Princess Leilani in the breast.
After chasing the assassin into the forest,
Frederic paused and listened, while horses
Galloped away. When Frederic emerged from
The woods, Marsha Moss was kneeling beside
Princess Leilani, weeping, because she lay
Motionless, as her life bled on the ground.
Suddenly, the Governess saw him there, and
Yelled to the guards, saying, "Arrest King
Frederic, who murdered my beloved mistress!"

Afterward, as King Alto and his parliament
Were in session, seated at the round table,
Which had become famous throughout Alettas
For the ways in which it dealt out justice,
Soliciting free education for all citizens,
And laws that made their nation prosperous,
The meeting was interrupted by Marsha Moss,
Who explained what happened, and then went
With King Alto to see Princess Leilani who
Lay on the bed, quite still and motionless,
Somewhere in between life and death itself,
Yet conscious of hearing King Alto's words,

When he said, "Leilani wake up and look at
Your father. Is this the man who shot you
With an arrow?" Suddenly opening her eyes,
As wide as saucers, because her father had
Accused and pointed his finger at Frederic,
Princess Leilani said, "No, he is innocent.
The man who would murder me was with Count
Darby this morning; he and not Frederic is
The one who skewered me with a cruel arrow."
Without delay, King Alto helped his guards
To remove the shackles from their prisoner.
When Frederic stood up, he stunned the two

Physicians by asking King Alto if he could
Have his permission to retrieve some fruit
From the Tree of Life, in his bedroom, and
Then prepare it for his daughter, Princess
Leilani. "How can you heal Leilani, after
My personal Physicians have worked in vain?"
King Alto said and not without good reason,
Since what Frederic had proposed to do was
A thing unknown to them, still. "Trust me,"
Frederic said to King Alto. "This is holy
Fruit that has come down from Heaven." So
King Alto agreed, and said, "Bring it here."

But, when Frederic returned with the fruit
From the Tree of Life, the Physicians grew
Irritated, and would not let him come near
The Princess, and they uttered a complaint
To King Alto, saying, "We protest, this is
Witchcraft he practices, not pure medicine."
It was then that King Alto lost his temper,
And then shouted at the learned Physicians,
Saying, "Would you rather my daughter died!
You've tried all of your medical knowledge,
Bled, prodded, puked, burned and blistered.
There's nothing left in your bag of tricks!

So I say to you, let Leilani eat the fruit."
The Physicians knew at once they must obey
His command, and they stood out of the way,
While Frederic squeezed the fruit juice in
A glass and then raised Princess Leilani's
Head, so that she could drink from the cup.
Then everyone was amazed, since the moment
Frederic applied the poultice to her chest,
Princess Leilani's wound healed, instantly.
Now the Physicians talked among themselves,
Because the fruit would make them rich men.
Then they turned to Frederic and asked him,

"Sir, where might we go to find this fruit?"
But Frederic knew their hearts and he said,
"Soon, you will cease to profit from human
Sorrows. This holy cure I shall give away,
First to the Ardenians, to whom this fruit
Belongs, and then to the rest of the world."
This caused the Physicians to grumble, and
When departing from the chamber, they said
Frederic should have his head examined for
Lunacy. After they left, Princess Leilani,
Who had never felt better, said she wanted
Everyone to hear a strange, mystical story.

"While I lay in dread, dying from my wound,
Something happened, I can't easily explain.
I found myself lost, inside of a dark cave,
Where lots of things crawled under my bare
Feet, such as snakes and spiders and worms.
There, I smelled a stench worse than death.
I felt afraid, just as if abandoned by God.
After leaving the cave, I stood at a cliff,
Where a road sign hovered in the air, with
A picture of Satan's horns and these words
Written on it: These are the Gates of Hell.
Souls who pass here can never return again.

Right about then, I heard loud noises, and
Turning around, I saw an ugly monster, who
Smiled, and then ripped off one of my arms,
Which, to my surprise, grew back instantly.
As the monster tore off my arm, repeatedly,
And watched it grow back again, I believed
It would enjoy hurting me for all eternity,
If another monster, even more hideous than
The first, had not stretched out a big paw
The size of a pitchfork and then clawed my
Stomach, quickly disemboweled me, and then
Pushed me over the edge of the steep cliff.

As I fell into the abyss, I reached out to
Grab the branch of a withered dwarfed tree
That grew below, on the side of that cliff,
Knowing that whole time if my hand slipped
From that dried and lifeless branch that I
Would wind up in Hell, and be lost forever.
Just then, shaking with terror and fear, I
Cried out to the Lord, 'Jesus save my soul!'
Then suddenly, Jesus caught me in his arms
And then flew with me to a place in Heaven.
We spoke, but I can't recall what was said.
Then I awoke, back inside of my body again."

King Alto felt grateful since Frederic had
Worked a miracle by saving the life of his
Only daughter, and he said, being generous,
"What may I give you as a reward, a parcel
Of good land, or maybe you would like gold?
I'll award whatever you want, just name it."
Now the time had come for Frederic to tell
King Alto his reason for coming to Alettas,
So he said, without hesitation, "King Alto,
I have come here for one reason only, so I
Could find the ruby belonging to the Sword
Of Tarsus, and take it to my home in Arden.

A ruby adorns an ancestral crown displayed
In the lobby. I want this to be my reward."
But King Alto thought this reward unworthy,
And said, "No, my daughter's life is worth
More than a gem; please choose more wisely."
When Frederic said, "It is the ruby I want,"
King Alto said Frederic was being stubborn.
Then he shrugged. "All right, it is yours,"
He said, relenting, "let's go to the lobby."
But Frederic insisted he take the Sword of
Tarsus with him, so he went to his room to
Fetch the sword, before going to the lobby.

There, he met King Alto, who stood looking
At the display case for a moment, and said,
"Since there are many crowns from which to
Choose, and many rubies in each crown, how
Shall you know which one belongs to Tarsus?"
So Frederic replied, "Let the sword choose."
Then at that moment, as Frederic stretched
Out his arm, the Sword of Tarsus tugged on
The crown with the ruby, until, shattering
The glass, the crown flew across the floor
And then stopped just inches from his feet,
To the amazement of everyone who was there.

Bewildered, the servant rushed to pick up
The crown, until a worried Frederic waved
Him off with a sudden gesture of his hand.
"Don't touch it!" Frederic shouted to the
Servant, as the ruby itself began to glow
Red hot, melting the gold that secured it.
Then they watched, with total fascination,
When the ruby levitated upward in the air
And then moved sideways, until it hovered
Around the slot in the sword's hilt, then
Passed through it like thread in a needle.
All at once, the sword shook violently as

A shaft of light shot up through the roof,
At the same time three precious gemstones
On the hilt, one of green emerald, one of
Blue sapphire, and the other pink diamond,
Started to blink thrice and then went out,
Signifying a successful power restoration.
When activated, the Sword of Tarsus would
Come to the aid of anyone that wielded it.
This was a good thing, since Frederic ran
Outside on the palace lawn, where a dozen
Guards, with long spears, noisily shouted,
And then looking up, saw the black Dragon.

In fact, the Sword of Tarsus had summoned
The black Dragon, which quickly responded
In this way, by picking up big white ewes
In the pasture, and then dropping them on
The guards, who got splattered with blood,
And ducked to evade its long sharp talons.
Right then Frederic understood two things.
One, the black Dragon had come to destroy
The Sword of Tarsus, if it possibly could.
Two, it wanted the fruit from the Tree of
Life, that Frederic remembered leaving in
A pouch, up in Princess Leilani's bedroom.

When Frederic ran up the stairs, in front
Of the aged and infirm King Alto, he felt
That Princess Leilani was in grave danger.
But, when Frederic opened the door of her
Bedroom, while King Alto was looking over
His shoulder, he was relieved to see that
Princess Leilani lay in her bed, at peace.
Without wanting to disturb her, they soon
Turned around to leave, and that was when
It happened. They heard a deafening wail
And then saw the black Dragon, as it hung
From the eaves, upside down in the window.

Instantly, the black Dragon's long tongue,
Split like that of a snake, darted out of
Its mouth, because it caught the scent of
Fruit, that sweet fragrance of God, which
Wafted on the wind through an open window.
Frederic glanced down at the pouch, which
He had left on the desk near the bed, and
Said, "Leilani, quick, bring me the pouch!"
Suddenly a stunned Princess Leilani leapt
Out of bed, holding the pouch in her hand.
Seeing this the black Dragon grew enraged.
It puffed up both cheeks and then exhaled,

Blowing out a cloud of germs the Togalons
Had grown in a biological weapons factory.
When the early warning detected the germs,
Just then, a loud buzzing noise was heard,
While the emerald blinked on and then off.
On the instant Frederic pressed his thumb
On the emerald, a big ball of flames shot
From the Sword of Tarsus, and incinerated
All of the germs, before they had time to
Infect everyone; now, with a beak injured,
Burnt by searing flames, the black Dragon
Let out a loud screech and then flew away.

At six o'clock the next morning, Frederic
Put a few belongings in his leather pouch
And then went downstairs to eat breakfast
With King Alto and his daughter, Princess
Leilani, whose appearance had the blossom
Of health in springtime, ruddy and robust.
King Alto was sorry to see Frederic leave,
And said to him, "I know you are eager to
Return to Arden so you can take back your
Crown from Edmund who impudently wears it.
To this end, I pledge my aid and do offer
You half a dozen ships, all welled manned."

Right then, Frederic felt humbled by King
Alto's kindness, and said, "Your Grace, I
Have no money to pay you for these things.
You do this from great love for my father.
But one day, I promise to pay you in full."
After the two men embraced, Frederic went
Downstairs, where Princess Leilani waited
By the coach, hoping for a few moments of
Intimacy, before Frederic left the palace.
To his surprise, she hung a golden locket
Around his neck and then said, "Wear this
Locket, keep it close, next to your heart.

A long time from now, when you rule again
From the throne of Arden, and all of your
Memories have grown dull in forgetfulness,
Look on my locket and my likeness therein,
And recall, in pleasant sweet remembrance,
How this Princess cherished and loved you."
Frederic bowed and kissed her on the hand.
"You greatly honor me," he said. "I will
Carry your gift on my person at all times."
Then Frederic left in the coach and waved
To her out the window, and said, "Goodbye,
Leilani, and I hope we meet again one day."

BOOK THREE

Frederic sailed to the country of Arden by
Ship, paying his passage with money loaned
To him by King Alto, who would send half a
Dozen ships of war later on, whenever they
Were asked for by Frederic, who arrived at
Arden, six weeks later, in the Port of Poe.
After that Frederic bought a good horse in
The market on the square, and then began a
Journey by which he avoided the main roads,
By traveling at night, sleeping in the day
Next to a campfire, so none would know him
And turn him into King Edmund for a reward.

One day, near the old town of Williamsburg,
When several miles from Longhengren Castle,
He came upon an old woman, in the twilight
Of dusk, carrying a heavy sack of potatoes
On her misshapen hunched back, in the hope
She would sell them at the farmer's market.
"Sir, please lighten my burden, and buy my
Potatoes, which no one in town bought from
Me, although I spent all day at the market.
You'll find no black molds or rotten sores
On my potatoes, picked yesterday, which is
More than I can say for our cursed country."

Frederic then took pity upon the old woman,
Who had warts on her face and spoke with a
Sucking lisp because of her toothless gums.
"Give me two pound, Frederic said, putting
In her thin withered hand a coin worth far
More. "You may keep the change good woman."
Suddenly, Frederic knew that he had made a
Mistake when the old woman squinted at him,
And said, "You must be manor born, and fed
With a silver spoon, to think so little of
Money. I believe your face looks familiar.
I wonder now, where have I seen you before?"

When the old woman leaned her head forward,
Then peered directly at his face, Frederic
Quickly pulled his hood down over his eyes,
Trying to avoid her gaze, and then replied,
"It is possible that you've seen me before,
Since I once lived nearby, a long time ago."
Now hoping to change the subject, Frederic
Tied the sack to his saddle, and then said,
"Tell me old woman, where does King Edmund
Reside, today; is he at Longhengren Castle?"
The old woman eyed Frederic with suspicion.
"It is a queer thing which you ask me, sir."

Frederic thought he'd made another mistake,
And said, "Why, when my words are ordinary?"
The old woman said, "Perhaps you are a spy?
Everybody knows where the evil King abides."
Hoping to ease her mind, Frederic said, "I
Hasten there, on business with King Edmund."
"Your business is none of my affair. This
Road shall bring you to Longhengren Castle
Where King Edmund sits like a pompous toad
On his throne, all dressed in fine clothes,
Like the eyed feathers of a garden peacock.
There you'll find him with elegant damsels."

Frederic became favorably impressed by the
Old crone, and he said, "I see that you're
Not afraid of King Edmund like most people."
As she scratched several hairs on her chin,
The old crone replied, "I'm more afraid of
Thieves in the forest who rob and steal or
Take a sudden dislike, and cut your throat.
Once, these murderers were gentle soldiers
Of King Frederic, God bless his soul. Bad
As he was, he seemed ten times better than
His brother, Edmund, the envious evil King.
Heed my advice, avoid danger in the forest."

But, Frederic ignored this warning, and he
Parted from her, speaking these last words,
"Goodday to you, Madame." With suspicions
Aroused, the old vagabond said to Frederic,
"This day is nearly over, and night begins.
Therefore I say goodnight, and not goodday."
Continuing on down the same road, Frederic
Quickened the pace of his horse, for three
Miles, until he paused by some thick woods
Where light struggled to pierce the canopy,
In which he could hear birds singing songs,
Though the birds themselves were invisible.

Suddenly, like the old woman had predicted,
Frederic was ambushed by four robbers, who
Surprised him, by jumping from the thicket,
Holding the leather reins, and pulling him
From the saddle, so that he fell very hard,
And hit the side of his head on the ground.
When struggling to get back up on his feet,
Frederic could hardly believe his ears, in
That he recognized the voice of his Knight,
Sir Chester Dune, telling him to surrender
His purse. Then Frederic shouted the name
Of his Knight who was loyal once, and said,

"I, King Frederic, call you mad barbarians
For sinking so low as to rob all travelers!"
This provoked Sir Chester Dune into saying,
"Who are you to impersonate our noble King?
Frederic's a better man than you, the best
Man to have ruled over the nation of Arden!"
It was then when Frederic removed his hood,
All of a sudden, that Sir Chester Dune saw
The face of his King, and then fell to his
Knees in awe, and said to Knights with him,
"This is King Frederic; Almighty God heard
Our prayers; he comes to reclaim his crown!"

When Frederic saw that all of his Knights
Had traded in their practiced virtues for
The easy vices of thieves who wait beside
The road to steal from innocent travelers,
He grew greatly troubled in his heart and
Then said to his friend, Sir Chester Dune,
"How is it that you, a virtuous Knight of
The realm, can tumble from Heaven to Hell?
It seems as if you emulate a fallen Angel,
By copying all of the robbers and thieves,
Who line their pockets with stolen silver.
Have you no defense to win over your King?"

Frederic's words seemed to cut the Knight
Down to the bone, since he flinched as if
In great pain, and then said, "Everything
Has changed in your absence, sire. These
Are most desperate times in which we live.
Edmund has put off our nation's just laws."
But Frederic remained firm, and said, "As
Long as I'm King, you'll stop acting like
A band of thieves. Do you all understand?"
Sir Chester Dune bowed his head, and said,
"Sire, soldiers are coming. Edmund's men
Search everywhere on the roads to find us."

Quickly, they left the road and then went
To hide in the woods, where they remained
Motionless, silent in the grove of spruce,
Until the fast paced riders had passed by.
After that, they started out for the camp
That was located upon the bank of a river,
Whose natural cliffs made of granite rock
Were a great height, massive, impregnable,
Like the stonewalls of Longhengren Castle.
From the ramparts, they noticed sentinels
Waving to them in recognition and kinship.
This signal meant they should go in peace.

On his arrival at camp, Frederic was given
A fine spacious cabin made out of logs, in
Which he slept that night in great comfort.
Bright and early the next morning, he held
A Council of War, in which former officers
Brought him up to date with current events.
Among those who sat at the high table were
Lord Dune and General Killarney, who spoke
First, while others listened to his report.
"Each day more and more of our people turn
Against Edmund, and come to fill our ranks.
Blacksmiths can't make weapons fast enough."

After that Lord Dune spoke to them, saying,
"Circumstances are more favorable now than
They were previously. The Pazmanians came
To realize they cannot trust Edmund, after
He had promised to share with them half of
The fruit, and then shipped nothing at all."
General Killarney spoke again, "They hated
Edmund for stealing the black Dragon right
From under their noses; they accuse him of
Taking the only control box, and of moving
The black Dragon inside Longhengren Castle,
Where it is locked up, within an iron cage."

Wishing not to be outdone, Lord Dune spoke,
And said, "In my opinion, there is no need
To worry about whether the Pazmanians will
Come to help Edmund, whose underhanded and
Disingenuous methods have alienated all of
His former friends who had come to his aid."
"How did you come by this good information?"
Frederic asked General Killarney, who said,
"Fortunately, there is a spy in the castle:
Your stable boy Tom Hutchins, who comes to
Tell us things. O look, here he comes now!
What news shall he bring concerning Edmund?"

When they were through greeting each other,
General Killarney spoke first, and said to
Tom Hutchins, who had turned only nineteen
The prior month, on the tenth day of April,
"What dark evil lies festering in the mind
Of Edmund, who remains close to his castle?"
"Well, much has happened since we last met,
Four weeks ago," Tom Hutchins said, slowly.
"Since then, Edmund has uncovered a secret
Plot, when some officers tried to kill him,
Due to his madness. But, they have failed
Because of General Rudolph, who learned of

The insurrection, and surprised the rebels,
Who contemplated murder while Edmund slept."
When Lord Dune asked, "What happened after
The rebels were caught?" Tom Hutchins said,
"When Edmund was told, his heart boiled in
Rage, and he searched throughout the realm
To find other accomplices, and then hanged
Ten officers tried on suspicion of treason.
The castle has become unsafe, since Edmund
Now suspects everyone of wanting to murder
Him. I really don't know what will happen.
Each day, Edmund becomes more like a demon."

Now Frederic was worried for the safety of
His family, who were imprisoned in certain
Rooms of the castle. When all of them had
Gone, Frederic sat down at a desk to write
A letter to Kathleen, saying he planned to
Rescue everybody from the castle, tomorrow,
Near midnight, during a time that would be
Least likely to arouse suspicion, and when
The majority of Edmund's soldiers would be
Asleep. Meanwhile, Tom Hutchins waited in
The next chamber, since he would take this
Letter on his return to Longhengren Castle.

When he had written his letter to Kathleen,
Frederic held a candle over the paper, and
Then poured out a gob of melted wax, which
He pressed and sealed with the King's ring.
"Keep this letter a secret," Frederic said,
"My officers will stop me if they find out."
"I will tell no one," Tom Hutchins replied.
On handing over the letter, Frederic added,
"Be careful, they will hang you if you are
Caught." When answering him, Tom Hutchins
Said, "I'd give all that I have, including
My life, if it helps to depose this tyrant."

Soon afterward, Tom Hutchins left the camp,
With Frederic's letter stuffed in his coat,
And headed in the direction of Longhengren
Castle. When half way there, Tom Hutchins
Became frightened and then hid in the wood,
Believing soldiers were searching the road.
However, as they drew near and he saw they
Were farmers, hauling vegetables to market,
Tom Hutchins hurried to find Kathleen, who
Sat in a drawing room, reading from a book.
After breaking the wax seal, Kathleen read
The words that Frederic scribbled in haste.

"I shall be at Longhengren Castle tomorrow,
At midnight; be prepared to fly from there."
Now surprised by the letter, Kathleen said,
"I have heard no news since I have been in
These walls, which are like an ivory tower.
It is true, Frederic resides back in Arden?"
As soon as Tom Hutchins said, "Yes, Madame,
Frederic told me to give this letter to no
One but you," Kathleen said, "Then we must
Stop Frederic, since guards are everywhere.
I fear they set a trap. Wait for my reply,
Which you are to take to Frederic, at once."

When Kathleen returned again, Tom Hutchins
Stuffed her letter in his pocket, and then
Journeyed to the stable, to put his saddle
On a fresh horse, the other being fatigued.
Unfortunately, Edmund waited here, flanked
By hooded men, cruel sadists and torturers.
"Are you leaving somewhere in a hurry, Tom?"
Edmund asked in a hard tone of voice. Not
Waiting for Tom Hutchins to answer, Edmund
Spoke to these two villains, and then said,
"Search him for Kathleen's letter! I know
That he carries one. The new maid told me."

In the great hall, Kathleen sat at a table,
With her twelve year old daughter, Jasmine.
Sitting right across from her was Gertrude,
Frederic's mother, who soon came to resent
The fact that Edmund was late and Kathleen
Was afraid to start the supper without him.
"Edmund knows the hour when we have supper,"
Gertrude said. "I remember if Edmund came
Late to the table as a child, I would make
Him go to bed, hungry, hoping to teach him
A valuable lesson. You just can't imagine
How harshly I had to spank Edmund's bottom."

Right then Edmund walked in the great hall,
And stopping near the entrance, he shouted
To Kathleen, saying, "Come here, I wish to
Have a word with you in private!" However,
A feeling of dread came over Kathleen, who
Stayed seated, afraid of leaving the table.
"Did you think you could write a letter to
Frederic and then keep it a secret from me?"
Edmund said. "What letter?" Kathleen said,
Feigning innocence. "Well, if this letter
Isn't yours," Edmund said, teasing her now,
"Then you probably won't care if I read it."

Edmund then slid a hand inside of his coat
To remove the folded letter which Kathleen
Had written in haste to warn Frederic away
From Longhengren Castle. After opening it,
Edmund read the letter to everyone, saying,
"Dear Frederic, I know your love for me is
The reason that you risk your life to save
Us from Edmund, who grows increasingly mad.
But be well advised, the thing you propose
Would be reckless indeed. Do not think of
Coming here at the appointed midnight hour,
Since guards incessantly watch the grounds."

Suddenly Kathleen made an attempt to steal
The letter, but Edmund quickly stopped her
When he pushed on her shoulder, and shoved
Her back down in the chair. When she made
A second effort to leave the table, Edmund
Held her there by pulling back on her hair.
Just then they were interrupted by Jasmine,
Kathleen's only child by her first husband,
Malcolm, the great Knight errant. Jasmine
Had grown tired of their endless arguments.
Now wanting to go outside, Jasmine said to
Kathleen, "Mother I don't feel like eating.

I want to play with Sam. May I be excused?"
Sam was her white miniature spaniel. "Yes,"
Kathleen said, hoping to keep her daughter
Away from Edmund. "Stay on the front lawn."
But, Edmund saw through her scheme, and he
Said, "No, I think you should stay Jasmine.
Kathleen wants to explain the mystery that
Surrounds your father's disappearance, and
Untimely death." "Is there a secret, Uncle
Edmund?" Jasmine asked. Feeling horrified
Edmund might tell the truth, Kathleen said,
"No, Jasmine! Please run outside and play!"

After Jasmine had departed the great hall,
Kathleen spurned Edmund, with a vengeance,
Saying, "Be silent, Edmund! Jasmine must
Never know the malignant lie that gossips
Whisper at court, hoping to hurt Frederic,
And turn him against our vows of marriage."
Now taken aback by her fury, Edmund asked,
"But how do we know if the rumor is a lie?
Although some say Frederic loves humanity,
I believe that his character has a darker
Side and that he loves doing wicked deeds.
Yet, none of this matters since I am King.

Everything that belonged to him, his land,
His castle, and his people, do now belong
To me. This includes you, his horny wife."
Just then Edmund ground his mouth against
Kathleen's teeth, hurting her lips. When
She fought to break out of Edmund's grasp,
Kathleen lunged and slapped Edmund across
The face, leaving a red mark on his cheek.
"You presumed too much, Edmund!" Kathleen
Said, "I'll never come to lie in your bed!"
In reaction to that stinging blow, Edmund
Drew back a ways, and rubbed a sore cheek.

"I wouldn't deny my rights, if I were you,"
Edmund said to Kathleen. "I predict that
You will lie next to me in my bed one day,
Not because I shall make you, but because
You'll desire it, from your own free will."
"Never!" Kathleen cried, and she went out.
Then Gertrude stood up to leave the table.
"Are you leaving me mother?" Edmund asked,
Suddenly feeling betrayed. Gertrude felt
Depressed. "Right now I hate you, Edmund,"
She said, on leaving the room. "Frederic
Is twice the man you are, or ever will be!"

Edmund Discovers A Nest Of Dragons

That very next day, in the afternoon, when
Edmund busily posted guards all around the
Palace yard, in preparation for Frederic's
Arrival, now scheduled for twelve midnight,
According to the letter he had intercepted
From Kathleen, Edmund discovered something.
This with the help from a young guard, who
Had wandered into the woods to relieve his
Bladder, only to look down and then find a
Large nest, with half a dozen baby Dragons,
In various stages of breaking out of their
Hard shells twice the size of ostrich eggs.

From a sense of fear, Edmund turned around,
Since the black Dragon may be watching him.
To his great relief, Edmund saw no sign of
The mother, which he had sent on a mission
To terrorize the village of Freedom, after
Its citizens rose in rebellion against him.
So Edmund bent down and then picked up one
Egg with a baby Dragon peering from a hole,
And then carried it carefully in his hands,
All the way down to the big manicured lawn,
Where he showed the baby Dragon to Jasmine,
Who tossed a ball to her miniature spaniel.

Right after that Edmund went in the palace
To show his mother, Gertrude, who said the
Small reptile looked hideous, and she told
Him to take it away. Because Kathleen had
Gone to sleep in her chamber, after having
Complained of a headache, Edmund went down
The corridor and then turned into his room.
Once there, he set the large egg on top of
A bureau intricately inlaid with rare wood,
And then watched, as the baby dragon poked
A wider hole in the dome with an egg tooth,
And opened its mouth to be fed like a bird.

After about fifteen minutes, Edmund looked
Up and saw Kathleen hurry into his chamber.
There was a look of horror on her face, as
She panted, trying to catch her breath for
A moment, before she asked Edmund for help,
Saying, "That Dragon wants to kill Jasmine."
Edmund instantly knew what happened and he
Rushed to throw open the shutter, and then
Looked westward, over the tall garden maze,
Decorating the lawns of Longhengren Castle.
The black Dragon had unexpectedly returned
To the nest and then found Jasmine playing

With her babies and then had chased her up
The trunk of a willow, where she had clung
To the branches and then screamed for help.
"Do something!" Kathleen shouted to Edmund.
But Edmund wasn't in a hurry and he stared
At Kathleen who had just come from her bed,
Wearing her slippers and night gown, still.
So Edmund slowly reached out with his hand
To touch Kathleen's long blonde hair first,
And in the same movement touched her cheek,
Then ran his fingers down along her breast,
Making Kathleen jump backward, in surprise.

"Help Jasmine," Kathleen said, now feeling
Somewhat stimulated over Edmund's advances.
"Yes of course," Edmund said, as he walked
Forward and made Kathleen take a few steps
Backward to where the large King sized bed
Rested against one wall over in the corner.
Edmund gave Kathleen a lascivious, leering
Stare, and said, "First, we shall consider
The order of our priorities; I aid Jasmine
By stopping the black Dragon, then you aid
Me by coming to my bed." Quickly, Jasmine
Yelled again. "I am yours," Kathleen said.

After opening a window beside the bedstead,
Edmund removed the small black control box
From his coat and then pressed on the knob.
The black Dragon immediately responded, by
Lifting its wings in a graceful arc, which
It then lowered over its head, like a roof.
With the black Dragon suddenly immobilized,
Edmund set the control box down, on top of
The windowsill, intent on leaving it there.
Kathleen put up no resistance, and swooned
When Edmund picked her up in his arms, and
Then laid her upon the mattress of his bed.

This is what Edmund had expected, had told
Her would happen, even though she wouldn't
Believe him, and had resisted him at first.
Meanwhile, the baby Dragon sat on a bureau
And cried like a bird, wanting nourishment,
Sweet tender flesh from young virgin girls.
It was the same afternoon, two hours later,
When the twelve-year-old Jasmine, with her
Elderly grandmother, Gertrude, wandered in
Edmund's chamber, to unexpectedly discover
Edmund and Kathleen lying naked on the bed,
Covered with sheets like two peas in a pod.

Gertrude felt shocked at seeing them sleep
Together, and she soon pushed Jasmine from
The chamber, albeit quietly, trying not to
Disturb them from dreams of God knows what.
Later on, Edmund woke up and left the room,
With Kathleen still asleep on the mattress.
A few minutes later, when Kathleen woke up,
With the inevitable stigma of shame, after,
She went to her chamber to get dressed and
Then went out to stroll around on the yard,
Hoping to find Edmund, or Jasmine, who she
Had abandoned in favor of Edmund's passion.

First thing, Kathleen instinctively sought
The horse stables, where she hoped to find
Jasmine who frequently made trips there to
See her fifteen-year-old friend, a servant
Girl, with the name of Rosalind, who would
Help to exercise and groom the many horses.
As Kathleen wandered inside of the stables,
She suddenly froze, when she looked up and
Then saw the body of Tom Hutchins, hanging
From a rafter, his elbows tied together by
A rope, his face smeared with blood, after
Someone thoroughly beat him black and blue.

"O my God, what have they done to you, Tom?"
Kathleen said, when she touched one of his
Bare feet, and saw Tom was still breathing,
Still alive, as he winced from the pain of
Two broken legs, and looked at her through
Swollen eyes to express a sad little smile,
When he remembered Frederic, and then said,
"Does the King still come later on tonight?"
Kathleen appeared worried. "Yes Tom," she
Said. "But, I wish the opposite were true."
"Then I ask you one last favor before I go
Up yonder to see Jesus," Tom Hutchins said.

"Tell the King, when he finally appears, I
Never told those bastards what they wanted
To know, even though they tried their best
To break me. I've kept all of our secrets.
Will you tell him?" Tom Hutchins whispered.
Kathleen began to cry. "Of course, I will
Tell him for you," Kathleen replied. "Good,"
Tom Hutchins said. "Now I can go in peace."
Afterward, Tom Hutchins closed his eyelids
And then died. Soon, Kathleen heard a man
Coming, his heavy boots hitting the boards.
Whirling around, she fled from the stables.

Kathleen Is Appalled By Jasmine

Continuing on with her search for Jasmine,
Kathleen had a hunch, she would find both
Girls near the Dragon's nest, on the back
Lawn of the castle. Passing with caution,
Kathleen wandered by the black Dragon, as
It stood proud and immobile like a statue.
Kathleen still didn't know how Edmund had
Made it become inactive, only temporarily,
And she feared what she didn't understand.
Then, at the top of a knoll, a short ways
In the woods, Kathleen saw the large nest
Where both girls played with baby Dragons.

Fearing that the black Dragon might awake
From some deep sleep, at any given moment,
Kathleen urged the two girls to come away
From the nest, saying, "The mother Dragon
May hurt you; come along now, Edmund says
It eats the flesh from young virgin girls."
Jasmine's sudden response caught Kathleen
By surprise. "We are not virgins anymore,
So we needn't worry about that old Dragon,"
Jasmine said. Hoping to flaunt this fact,
Jasmine and Rosalind kissed each other on
The lips, which showed they were lesbians.

On the instant, Kathleen felt appalled by
What she believed to be shameful behavior,
And seeing as how Jasmine was now too big
To spank over her knee, Kathleen suddenly
Turned and then walked down to the castle,
Thinking she will talk to Edmund about it.
But once there, Kathleen found Edmund was
In no mood to speak since he had lost the
Box of controls used for the black Dragon.
Feeling upset, and bothered by a migraine,
Kathleen went in to take a nap. When she
Woke up again, Edmund was in her thoughts.

Kathleen quickly dressed, and then hurried
Down to the great hall, knowing Edmund got
Mad if she was late for meals at the table.
In a moment, Edmund said, "A family should
Talk and then share things; let's begin by
Having Jasmine tell us what she did, today."
Jasmine glanced coldly at Edmund, and said,
"I spent it with my friend, Rosalind. Why?"
Then Edmund said, "Your mother has told me.
She thinks you and this servant are queers."
Soon, Jasmine retorted, "No, we are lovers,
And not incestuous like you and mother are."

Just then Edmund grew angry at Jasmine and
Shouted, "Now what's that supposed to mean!"
So, Jasmine said, "Grandma and I walked in
While you were both lying naked on the bed."
Gertrude squirmed in her chair, and wished
Jasmine remained quiet; suddenly, Kathleen
Said, "If I had known that beforehand, you
Can bet I would not have slept with Edmund.
I tried to keep the Dragon from eating you."
Baiting Kathleen Edmund said, "All of this
Time I thought it was because you loved me."
Gertrude couldn't take it anymore, and she

Started to leave. But before she did, she
Rebuked Edmund and said, "Kathleen told me
You had Tom Hutchins tortured and murdered.
You've always been a cruel monster, Edmund.
I wish I had aborted you, torn you from my
Womb, while you were a babe, as yet unborn."
Suddenly, Edmund grew furious, and shouted,
"I don't care what you do! You and father
Had two sons, and yet you favored Frederic.
Nothing in the world matters to me anymore,
As I, Edmund, now wear the crown of a King.
Depart from me, you pit of venomous vipers!"

It was much later on, while Kathleen stood
On the white marble balcony, looking up at
The soft velvet night, with moon and stars,
That she heard quick footsteps coming from
Behind her, then suddenly turned around to
See Edmund, weaving unsteadily on his feet.
Kathleen froze, since instinct told her to
Be afraid of Edmund, who grew violent when
Inebriated. Slowly, Edmund approached her,
Carrying the half empty bottle in his hand,
Of good red wine, when he suddenly shouted,
Bellowed loudly like a bull, and then said,

"I've looked everywhere for my small magic
Box, which I need to make the black Dragon
Obey my commands. I believe you've hidden
It from me. Tell me where, before I start
To lose my patience." Edmund paused, then
Drank, with the bottle tipped at his mouth.
"Honestly, Edmund," Kathleen said, "I have
No idea where you put the magic box. It's
Probably right where you left it." Edmund
Slapped Kathleen on the face with his hand.
"Don't sass me," Edmund said. "Lies, even
Pretty ones, can prove bad for your health."

Then suddenly, something dramatic happened.
Soon, Frederic stepped out from behind one
Of the long curtains, holding the Sword of
Tarsus in his hand, blinking a green light.
"Why don't you fight a man!" Frederic said,
Rather sternly, as he rushed toward Edmund.
It was hard to tell who was more surprised
To see Frederic standing there, Edmund, or
Kathleen. But, it was Edmund who drew out
His sword, and made a thrust in Frederic's
Direction, which Frederic easily countered,
By batting his sword clear across the room.

Now the sword went clanging over the tiles,
As Edmund quickly spun around on his heels
And ran down the flight of stairs, yelling,
"Come guards, Frederic is here, arrest him!"
Frederic repressed an urge to chase Edmund.
Instead, he turned around to hold Kathleen,
Who shrank from his touch, all of a sudden,
Saying, "No, you remind me of Edmund. You
Don't know what Hell I've experienced just
Being in this same castle with that rotten
Bastard." Frederic could see Kathleen was
In shock, and asked her to find the others.

They were in luck, since his mother waited
With Jasmine in an adjourning chamber, and
Came out to see him, as soon as Edmund had
Gone. Frederic spoke, but only to say, "I
Think we ought to use the servant's stairs.
Edmund will bring his soldiers, any minute."
So they headed down for the lobby, just as
They heard Edmund and his guards ascending
Up the main staircase, which they suddenly
Descended again, when they came to realize
What had happened. In a matter of minutes,
The two groups met each other in the lobby.

This they were able to do because Gertrude,
Aged and infirm, had slowed their progress.
"Go outside to wait for me," Frederic said,
As he turned to meet Edmund who had leaped
From the bottom step, with new sword drawn,
Just a few seconds ahead of a dozen guards.
Suddenly, the warning system buzzed loudly,
While the pink diamond blinked, on and off,
Until Frederic pressed on the gem with his
Thumb and then watched, as lightning bolts
Shot from the Sword of Tarsus, and quickly
Paralyzed those men, who fell on the floor.

Frederic crossed himself and said a prayer,
Without knowing they were only temporarily
Stunned, and were not dead, as he believed.
When going outside to meet with the others,
He could sense their wild excitement, when
Jasmine mentioned the nest of baby Dragons.
The news alarmed everyone, and so Frederic
Insisted they find it, so he could destroy
The baby Dragons before they grew up to be
The size of their mother, the adult parent,
Who waited near, somewhere in the darkness,
Although immobile now, and perfectly still.

When they had reached the edge of the wall,
They ran across the meadow, bending low at
The waist to keep out of sight from guards,
Who manned the tower, until they were safe,
In the tall grass on the edge of the woods.
Jasmine knew they would find the nest here,
So Frederic listened carefully in the dark,
Straining his ears, until he heard peeping,
The sounds of song birds, a few yards away.
This time the emerald had started to blink.
Suddenly, when Frederic pressed on the gem

With his thumb, flames shot from the Sword
Of Tarsus with a loud rushing roaring wind
That consumed the entire brood in the nest,
Turning everything to a pile of gray ashes.
Then Frederic asked Jasmine, "Where is the
Mother?" As Jasmine pointed with a finger
At the patch of woods, more than a hundred
Yards away, Frederic thought he could slay
The black Dragon; but, this was impossible,
Because there just wasn't enough time left.
Forty soldiers were coming from the castle,
Beating the bushes, and checking the walls.

Realizing they had to go, Frederic set out
Along the path that servants used each day,
Going back and forth to work at the castle.
Because they could not slow down, Frederic
Helped his elderly mother through the dark
Woods, dappled by shadows from a full moon.
After they had gone about a mile, Frederic
Stopped on the trail and then listened for
A moment in silence, straining his ears to
Hear if guards were gaining ground on them.
Luckily, Frederic could only hear the wind
As it blew through the pine scented forest.

After three miles, they waded upstream for
Ten yards, hoping to cover up their tracks.
It was around noontime, for the bright sun
Was directly overhead, when they came to a
Wide open field that was next to the woods.
Here they stopped to lie down in the grass.
Frederic felt tired, from too little sleep
Over the last few days, and so he shut his
Eyelids, and soon drifted into unconscious.
Now, without knowing how long he had slept,
For minutes or for hours, Frederic woke up,
Feeling the field shake like an earthquake.

Looking up in the sky, just then, Frederic
Saw the black Dragon, before everyone else,
As it banked on the air, carrying two more
Boulders, gripped within its strong talons.
This was when Kathleen said, "Edmund found
The control box, damn his soul all to Hell!"
And when Frederic said, "Make a run for it!"
Since Gertrude had sprained her ankle, and
Couldn't keep up, she leaned her weight on
Frederic's shoulder and then hopped across
The field; by the time they got there, all
Of the others were hiding within the trees.

For some reason, possibly out of fear, or
From too many distractions, Frederic only
Now heard the alarm, a loud buzzing noise,
Coming from the Sword of Tarsus, and then
Looked to find the blue sapphire blinking,
On and then off, giving its early warning.
Frederic had yet to see what secret power
The blue stone held in store, and so with
A feeling of eager anticipation, Frederic
Pressed the blinking light with his thumb,
Then paused a moment to see what happened.
But to his surprise, Frederic saw nothing.

By now the loud buzzing noise had stopped,
And yet the blue light continued to blink.
It was a sign that something had happened.
Just what, it was impossible for Frederic
To tell, he having never heard of stealth
Cloaking device, which operated invisibly.
But Frederic had noticed the black Dragon
Passing idly, unable to find the location,
And wondered if the sword had anything to
Do with it. Much to their surprise, in a
Few minutes more, the black Dragon let go
Of its missiles, dropping them miles away.

Then to their amazement, the black Dragon
Turned back toward Longhengren Castle and
Then quickly disappeared from their sight.
But, Frederic told everyone to stay where
They were, because the black Dragon could
Return with more boulders. An hour later,
They started out, keeping well within the
The forest, until, in the waning twilight,
They emerged from the trees to see an old
Farmhouse with crumbled walls and sagging
Roof; here, they took refuge from ominous
Dark storm clouds brooding over the hills.

They were all prepared to spend the night.
However, they had no luxuries to speak of,
Only a small glass jar to catch rainwater,
Which Frederic had found in a garbage pit.
Still, they drank from it to quench their
Thirst. And yet, without flint and steel
To make a fire, they shivered in the cold;
And without food to eat, they went hungry.
After a couple of hours of suffering like
This, Jasmine said to her mother, "I wish
I'd never left the comforts of the castle."
Kathleen said, "You don't mean that child."

"O yes, I do," Jasmine said. "I doubt if
Uncle Edmund would let that black monster
Hurt me. I doubt if he is as bad as that."
Feeling upset, Gertrude groaned, and said,
"Edmund's soul is like that black monster.
He doesn't care a thing about you Jasmine."
Just now, Kathleen remembered what it was
That she had wanted to tell Frederic. "No!
No!" Kathleen gasped, as she looked up at
Frederic in panic. "I forgot to tell you!
Edmund has kept a baby Dragon in his room.
He brought it in from the nest to show me."

Frederic felt shocked by this sudden news.
He stared in awkward disbelief for a time,
Wondering how Kathleen could forget about
Telling him something as important as the
Baby black Dragon, which he thought would
Grow up and come back to haunt his future.
Now Frederic looked up and saw his mother
Crawling on her stomach, eating the grass,
On which she choked, and spit out, saying,
"If cows and sheep eat grass, why can't I?
Grass is all I got for my supper, tonight.
Milk my teats, then put me out to pasture."

Gertrude Loses Her Mind

Understanding that his white haired mother
Had lost her sanity, or reached a breaking
Point, which happens frequently and is not
At all uncommon, when a person experiences
Too much suffering in life as Gertrude had,
Frederic helped her up and walked her back
To the shelter, where Gertrude said to him,
"I am a Queen, and a Queen should not have
To be in the cold, without her food or tea.
If you were a good son, you'd tell someone
To bring me my hat, slippers and nightgown.
I would rest within my own comfortable bed."

Frederic felt his heart breaking, and said,
"Mother, you know I would, if we were home."
Right then Gertrude looked dazed, and said,
"Not home? Then, where on earth am I, son?"
Frederic began to weep. "Since when do we
Call ruins home? Remember the golden days,
When you were married to my father, Harold?
You had a hundred servants at your command."
"I remember Harold," Gertrude said, as she
Laid her head on Frederic's lap and dreamt
Of ages past. "Men loved me for my beauty.
I had more suitors than any other princess.

How horrible it is to realize one day that
You've grown old, alone, useless to anyone!
I cry like a beggar, unwanted, and unloved!
Why should God call curses down on my head,
And want to punish me just because I'm old?"
Just then, when Gertrude cried out in pain,
Frederic lost patience, and said," But you
Are loved! I love you, Kathleen loves you!
Jasmine loves! Most of all, God loves you!"
In a moment, they gathered around Gertrude,
Who soon felt well or at least good enough
To fall asleep without dreaming bad dreams.

They Are Discovered By Soldiers

92

Now Frederic was startled, all of a sudden,
When he heard a dull buzzing noise, coming
From the Sword of Tarsus, and looking down
He saw, on the widest surface of the blade,
In a small rectangle, a series of pictures,
Which showed the location of his army camp.
Soaring far overhead in the thunder clouds,
Frederic could see the black Dragon riding
High on thermal drafts like a lone buzzard.
"Quick, everyone run and hide in the woods!"
Frederic shouted, while helping his mother,
Who limped on legs that wobbled like jelly.

Frederic couldn't explain how the Sword of
Tarsus could reveal these marvelous things.
No, he only knew he must do what it wanted,
When and where it wanted and how it wanted,
And that it wanted them to leave the house,
To search for his army, fifteen miles away.
There are moments when time seems to stand
Still, when the pace quickens and yet time
Slows down to a crawl, and comes to an end,
As though life itself had felt the eternal.
So did Frederic when he heard the sound of
Horses, followed by soldiers upon the road.

No longer needing to stare at the pictures,
Frederic shouted, "Praise God!" as soon as
He saw that honorable Knight, Chester Dune,
Cantering on the road, with a search party.
When Frederic stepped from the woods, they
Halted and then stared at him in disbelief.
Chester Dune felt overjoyed at seeing them,
And said, "Sire, we searched the roads day
And night, worried because Edmund's guards
Are looking for you." "Your courage makes
Me feel humble," Frederic said, "let us go
Back to camp before the black Dragon comes."

BOOK FOUR

Some months later, while living once again
Inside of their mountain retreat, Frederic
Met with his senior officers, in a Council
Of War, where they had many differences of
Opinion, on about everything under the sun,
None more than on the direction of the war.
But, their meeting was quickly interrupted
When an officer walked in the headquarters
Building to tell them that General Rudolph
Had arrived there at the camp to surrender
His sword, since he saw how corruption and
Chaos created inevitable defeat for Edmund.

"Bring him here," Frederic said, surprised.
"I'm sure that everyone wants to hear what
General Rudolph has to say, since he's the
Highest ranking officer who has come to us
Seeking defection, and what information he
Knows about King Edmund can be very useful."
Everyone turned their heads and watched as
General Rudolph made an official surrender,
By handing Frederic his sword and scabbard.
"It can't be easy for you, General Rudolph,"
Frederic said. "Why change your mind, now?
You could have surrendered many months ago."

"I erred in my desire for world domination,"
General Rudolph said. "I should have seen
Through Edmund's scheme sooner. I suppose
I became blinded by ambition. But at last,
I know that Edmund's unfit to rule as king,
After bringing only misery to this country.
I wish to tell you there are many citizens
Who believe the same way as I do, and that
They have formed secret groups who plan to
Resist Edmund, by fighting at every corner,
And at every field, and at every farmhouse,
Until his inglorious reign comes to an end."

"This is good news. I welcome resistance,
If it brings a quick end to this ugly war,"
Frederic said. "Now, let me turn to your
Fate. You have brought honor to yourself
When coming to surrender, General Rudolph.
This took courage and much soul searching.
Therefore, I'm prepared to be generous by
Limiting your confinement to the barracks.
After the war is over, you'll be released.
Right now I have other business to attend.
But I hope to see you on another occasion,
When we'll drink a glass of wine together."

General Rudolph bowed with deference like
A Prussian officer, and clicked his heels
Together. Instantly, he was taken out by
Two guards to a barracks, which served as
The prison quarters for captured officers.
After that, Frederic said to Chester Dune,
"Edmund's close circle of friends becomes
Smaller each day. Perhaps it's time that
We revive peace talks with the Pazmanians.
Recently, I was told by a reliable source
That King Hooligan hates Edmund, after he
Stole their black Dragon through trickery.

I also hear King Hooligan would do almost
Anything, if they could get back in their
Possession the black Dragon, they worship
Like a god. Since many of the Pazmanians
Crave fruit from the Tree of Life, he may
Accept those fair terms I made previously."
Chester Dune longed for adventure, and he
Said to Frederic, "When do we leave, sire?
I've always wanted to see Pazmania, whose
Rules and customs are so unlike any other
Country." Frederic smiled knowingly, and
Said, "Pack your bags. We leave tomorrow."

Meanwhile, as they sat on benches, crowded
In front of a large stone hearth, Gertrude
Revealed to Kathleen her serious doubts on
The quality of food and the rather austere
Conditions they had to put up with at camp,
When she said, "We have few comforts today!"
This upset Kathleen who busily knit a pair
Of socks for Jasmine; "Nonsense!" Kathleen
Said, "We have honey and biscuits and pots
Of hot brewed tea. More delights would be
Unwanted." But Gertrude insisted, and said,
"My feet are cold, the fire throws no heat.

I miss my cozy lodgings, and feel terrible,
Ever since Edmund stole Longhengren Castle."
Kathleen got angry when she heard Gertrude
Mention Edmund's name, and said, "Will you
Please stop complaining? We all miss home."
Feeling hurt, Gertrude quickly fell silent.
Seizing this moment to vex her grandmother,
Jasmine said, "I think Grammy would rather
Be back there in that old shack, where she
Shook and cried like a scared little mouse."
Gertrude stared coldly at Jasmine, who fed
Caged birds; with an expression of disdain,

She said, "I've every right to feel scared.
I'm daughter of a great King and wife of a
Great King. The title of Queen guarantees
My rights to the royal coffers. Would you
Have a Queen live on turnips like a pauper?
Too much idle talk has given me a headache."
Suddenly, Gertrude stood up, and then said,
Upon leaving the room, "I wish to lie down.
I felt a lot better, yesterday. But today,
I fear a relapse of my condition. Ouch! A
Sharp pain in my head! O have mercy, Lord,
On this poor pathetic frightened old woman!"

As soon as Gertrude had left their chamber,
Kathleen said to Jasmine, in a stern voice,
"Don't upset your grandmother whose nerves
Feel raw and exposed, like ulcerated teeth."
Suddenly, Jasmine put a finger in the cage,
And softly stroked one of the yellow birds.
"Mother, why do old people have bad nerves?"
Jasmine asked, without looking at Kathleen.
"Lots of reasons," Kathleen said. "People
Who grow old fear everything under the sun."
Then Jasmine said, "Mother, tell the truth.
Did you have my father killed, so that you

Could marry Frederic?" Feeling shocked by
Jasmine's question, Kathleen turned around,
Her brow knitted in a frown, when she said,
"I've told you, already. Why do you raise
This subject, again?" So, Jasmine replied,
"People whisper this at court; I hear them
As I walk by; is there truth in this rumor?"
"No!" Kathleen said. "Evil tongues spread
Rumors and they do it for just one purpose:
To demean our character for political gain.
Don't listen to gossips, whose tongues are
Honed sharper than the executioner's blade."

"But, it's a fact that you lay in Edmund's
Bed," Jasmine said, "this isn't just rumor."
Kathleen pursed her lips, and then replied,
"We've thoroughly aired this dirty laundry.
I hurt for your sake; I've nothing more to
Add; I forbid you to speak on this subject."
But Jasmine went on, without stopping, and
Said, "You knew I wanted to bring Rosalind
When we left Longhengren Castle that night.
Why didn't you tell Frederic?" Right then,
Kathleen grew melancholy, and said nothing.
This was the moment that Frederic appeared.

As Frederic came in the chamber, just then,
Kathleen said, "Jasmine wants to ask you a
Question." "You tattletale," Jasmine said.
Jasmine had said it, since she didn't want
Frederic to learn certain things about her
Relationship with her girlfriend, Rosalind.
"Then I'll tell him myself," Kathleen said.
"Jasmine would like to know why you didn't
Bring her girlfriend, on the night that we
Planned our escape from Longhengren Castle."
Frederic seemed puzzled. "What girlfriend
Is this?" Frederic asked, feeling dismayed.

"A girl by the name of Rosalind, who works
In your horse stables," Kathleen explained.
"They are lovers who hold hands and choose
Not to breed as stallion upon mare, but as
Mare to mare. As I happened on them, they
Were kissing one another in the back field."
Frederic became astonished. "This is most
Strange and unnatural," Frederic exclaimed.
"I'll ask my Physician to examine her; she
May only need a purge, a tincture of herbs,
Oil, vinegar, and salt to shock her system.
Soon, she will regain her physical balance."

Now Jasmine ran from the chamber, shouting,
"Why doesn't anyone understand me? I just
Want to be left alone!" When Frederic ran
After Jasmine, intending to bring her back,
He was halted by Kathleen, who said to him,
"The poor child feels confused, let her go!"
When Frederic returned, he draped his arms
Over Kathleen, kissed her on the lips, and
Said, "Why don't you draw a bath, and wait
Until I come to your room. Since you lost
Our last child through miscarriage, I wish
To beget a son before I leave for Pazmania."

Kathleen Decides To End Her Life

Obedient, Kathleen walked into her bedroom,
Where she told her two maids-in-waiting to
Make ready her bath. As soon as the maids
Poured hot water in the tub, and then laid
Her fresh nightgown on top of the mattress,
Kathleen released both maids, telling them,
"You may go; you have no other duties, and
Are free for the rest of the night." This
Pleased the two maids, who curtsied to her,
And then said, "Thank you, Madame, you are
Most kind. We'll only be a few doors away.
Please summon us if you need anything more."

When all alone again, Kathleen surrendered
To feelings of deep melancholy, and slowly
Undressed, letting her silken garment fall
To the floor. Then Kathleen appraised her
Naked body in the full length mirror, when
Putting her hands over the round baby bump.
"Frederic comes too late," Kathleen sighed,
Speaking only to herself. "For Edmund has
Come first, and sired this bastard child I
Carry in my womb, which can hardly be seen,
But soon will swell to the size of a melon.
The poor child is innocent and without sin."

Just then, Kathleen sat up in the tub, and
Then began to wash herself clean, all over.
"But, I have sinned before God, and I feel
No amount of scrubbing shall make me clean.
What trick does nature play inside my mind,
Since the more I scrub, the dirtier I feel?"
Just then Kathleen picked up a dagger from
The table, and then said, "May God forgive
My sins, and especially the sin of suicide."
Seconds later, Kathleen plunged the dagger
In her breast and then screamed. Fainting
From loss of blood, she became unconscious.

Just then, one of the faithful maids came
Back to ask Kathleen if she would require
Anything more of her, before she left for
The night. Suddenly, when the maid heard
Kathleen scream, she ran into the chamber,
Saying, "Why does my lady cry out in pain?"
In a few seconds, she found out why, when
She ran into the bathroom, and then found
Kathleen lying slumped over in the tub of
Hot water, stained crimson with her blood.
With a loud shriek, the maid suddenly ran
From the room to find someone to help her.

It happened that Frederic was coming down
The hall, just then, when he met the maid,
Who said, with a hysterical tone of voice,
"Master, come quick! Our lady lies dying
From a dagger wound, done by her own hand.
Some evil madness has taken over her mind!"
Without wasting a second, Frederic rushed
Into the bathroom, laid the blood smeared
Dagger on the table, and then said to the
Maid, "Help me to lay Kathleen on the bed."
Seconds later, Frederic ran from the room,
Only to return once again, this time with

A doctor, who thanked the clever maid for
Applying a cloth compress to stop further
Bleeding from the wound. The doctor, who
Had brought along a bag, containing fruit
From the Tree of Life, squeezed the juice
Into the wound, and covered it with fruit.
Then the powers of the fruit, whose aroma
Filled the room with the fragrance of God,
Healed Kathleen's dagger wound, instantly.
Feeling refreshed, Kathleen could see how
Sad their faces were, and said, "Merciful
Jesus, he saved me from God's great wrath!"

Remembering his own near death experience,
Frederic asked Kathleen a dozen questions,
"Did you see the Saints? Angels? Paradise?
Did you see Jesus inside of a long tunnel?"
Kathleen shook her head. "No, I ended up
In a dark place, where people just waited,
In silence, without looking at each other.
They seemed absorbed by the problems they
Had experienced on Earth, which they were
Compelled to remember over and over again,
Unable to forgive or forget their horrors,
Like lonely prisoners who sit in solitary.

There were some who wore ancient garments.
One man, in particular, who looked Middle-
Eastern, with his beard, turban, and robe,
Appeared to me like he was Judas Iscariot.
As I stood there and wondered wherefore I
Had come to this strange foreboding place,
I soon sensed a Heavenly presence near by,
And then saw two lights like bright stars,
Hovering near the outer edges of darkness.
Suddenly one light, larger than the other,
Grew angry with me, and then I understood:
The larger one was God, who shouted at me,

Not in words but with telepathic thoughts,
Saying, 'You did the worst thing possible!
You have destroyed my plans for your life!
Suicide has doomed you; now you must wait
Here with the others for my last judgment,
Which comes on the final day of the world!'
Just then, my soul shook in fear of God's
Punishment, which I no doubt now deserved.
Found guilty, I would receive the maximum
Sentence, and be cast into outer darkness,
Where I would wait, my soul dammed by God,
Until our destruction in the Lake of Fire."

Just then, Kathleen became distraught, and
Tears rolled down the sides of both cheeks,
Which gave her such a sad appearance those
Who were there started to weep in sympathy.
"What happened after that?" Frederic asked.
"Did you go to Hell?" "No," Kathleen said.
At this point Kathleen sobbed in her hands,
And then said, "Jesus acted as my advocate.
He then pleaded my defense to Almighty God,
And spoke on my behalf, with compassionate
Understanding for everything that I'd been
Through, beginning from when I was a child.

At first, they spoke with a normal tone of
Voice, but then, as they began to exchange
Opinions, I could no longer keep pace with
The speed of their conversation, that grew
In pitch and intensity, until suddenly, it
Ended with crescendos of lightning flashes.
When I looked again, I saw only Jesus, who
Loved me with unconditional love, and said,
"Our Heavenly Father has granted you mercy.
None will accuse you, except for the Devil.
Don't squander this second chance to begin
Your life anew. Leave me, and sin no more."

Now Frederic held Kathleen by the hand and
Then kissed her on the lips. Kathleen was
Like a glass, in need of being filled with
Water, and she kissed Frederic, once again.
Then Frederic said, "As I told you already,
I have to visit King Hooligan, in Pazmania.
Please do what the Physicians tell you and
Get plenty of rest. I must go, darling; I
Hope you don't feel lonesome when I'm gone."
Kathleen smiled. "I'll be fine," Kathleen
Said, "I'll stay with Jasmine and Gertrude."
When they went out, Frederic shut the door.

So Frederic began his journey for Pazmania,
Bright and early in the morning, as he set
Out on the road with several officers, who
Included Chester Dune, who was the bravest
Knight of the realm, and second Lieutenant
Malta, who only thought he was the bravest.
After four weeks of hard riding, they came
To the walls of Gunter, and then continued
To where King Hooligan lived in his palace,
A large structure made of sandstone, which
Boasted a big park with wild animals taken
From multiple locations all over the world.

However, when Frederic arrived before that
Palace, they were turned away at the gates
By a courtier, who said, speaking in words
That were like pidgin, "King Hooligan says
Me tell you not here. He has changed mind.
He regret you travel long ways for nothing."
As the courtier promptly departed, without
Explaining why this was, Frederic suddenly
Became irritated, and then went on down to
The next gate, and finding it unlocked, he
Went inside, with his small entourage, who
Soon found themselves in a splendid garden.

Now walking by beds of tulips and by pools
Of mirror like water, Frederic had admired
For calm serene reflections, they soon saw
The old gray haired man with wrinkled brow,
Who sat under one of the willow trees in a
Squat position, in sweet silent meditation.
Believing he might be one of the gardeners,
Frederic said, "I am here to meet with the
Great King Hooligan. Where may I find him?"
"Tell me, who are you?" the gardener asked.
"King Frederic of Arden." To his surprise,
The gardener said, "I am he, King Hooligan."

"You should've come through the front gate,"
King Hooligan said, being a stickler about
Formal protocol. "Yes, but we were turned
Away by a servant," Frederic said, annoyed.
"He said you weren't here, and furthermore
Had changed your mind on meeting us, today."
Just then King Hooligan looked puzzled, as
If he tried to remember something. "No, I
Never gave those orders to any of my staff,"
King Hooligan said, "but I'm glad you have
Let yourselves in the garden. My servants
Were being careless to leave the gate open."

Suddenly, they were startled by Ambassador
Bourbon, who appeared right out of nowhere,
In the company of eight palace guards, and
Then shouted, "Seize him, this is Frederic,
Brother to King Edmund, who puts a warrant
Out for his arrest, and a large reward too!"
Frederic was about ready to defend himself,
By drawing on the Sword of Tarsus, when he
Was suddenly rescued by King Hooligan, who
Shouted at Ambassador Bourbon, "Let him go!
Frederic has come as my guest, and as long
As he stays here, he shall be treated well!"

Being reluctant to comply with his release,
But knowing too he must obey King Hooligan,
Ambassador Bourbon led the guards away and
Then paused by the fountain, watching them.
Speaking a soliloquy, the Ambassador mused,
"Edmund is King, therefore I shall be King.
Tomorrow, King Hooligan and Prince Paragon
Shall be in the crowd, watching the parade,
Which celebrates our nation's independence.
As soon as they pass by before the gallery,
My assassins will attack these two despots,
Kill them, and bring their reign to an end."

Since Frederic had never met King Hooligan,
He became greatly surprised at finding the
Biggest warmonger, anywhere on this planet,
Had the appearance of a mild temple priest,
Who had just completed his evening prayers.
Just then, as Frederic tried to enter into
Talks, he was interrupted once again, this
Time by a young vigorous man King Hooligan
Introduced as Prince Paragon, who sat with
Legs crossed on woolen carpets, famous for
Their bright colors, ordering the servants
To bring them dinner, plenty of spicy food.

When Prince Paragon heard how Frederic was
Turned away at the front gate, he said, in
Apologetic tones, "There are ambitious men
At court, who oppose the rule of my father.
These rebels are liars, real troublemakers,
Who wish to stir the people into rebellion."
Frederic thought for a moment, and he said,
"Perhaps it is time you accept my original
Offer, which would give you ten percent of
The fruit from the Tree of Life." Shocked
By his revelation, Prince Paragon said, "I
Am confused by this news, of which we know

Nothing. I believe my father would accept
Such an offer if it were made." Just then,
Rage appeared as a dark storm cloud on the
Placid face of King Hooligan, who said, "I
Must speak to my Ambassador Ronald Bourbon.
He may be at the root of our missing fruit."
When King Hooligan sent a servant to bring
Ambassador Bourbon, so he can question him,
The servant reappeared, almost immediately,
With the news he had left the palace, in a
Hurry. "I thought as much," King Hooligan
Said. "Write out a warrant for his arrest."

When Frederic asked to hear the history of
The black Dragon, King Hooligan began with
This comment, and said, "Edmund lied to us.
Edmund deceived us when he stole the black
Dragon, after my people had given its name,
Aquilasaurus, which means the eagle lizard.
I wanted to make war on Edmund to get back
Our eagle lizard but my people were afraid.
They believed that Aquilasaurus had turned
Against them, since Edmund now had the box,
Without which, Aquilasaurus could not live.
Long before history, our people discovered

Aquilasaurus lying in a great sheet of ice
That had melted when the earth grew warmer.
Here also a small black box was discovered
Lying nearby in the mud. When we pushed a
Stick that looked like a mushroom, we were
Amazed, since Aquilasaurus knew how to fly.
Our people grew in awe of Aquilasaurus, so
We worshiped, and prayed to him like a god.
We sacrificed our children to Aquilasaurus,
Feeding him only tender young virgin girls.
In return for this, Aquilasaurus protected
Us from enemies, with a tireless vigilance."

Right then, Frederic stopped King Hooligan.
He said to him, "What if I told you that I
Could steal the black box from Edmund, and
Return the eagle lizard to you, once again?"
King Hooligan was shocked. "My people and
I would feel grateful," King Hooligan said.
Frederic now made his point. "If I return
The black Dragon, would you fight Edmund's
Army in the field in the same way that you
Helped Edmund to fight me?" King Hooligan
Shook Frederic by the hand, just then, and
Said, "Of course, on that you have my word."

Frederic had ended business at the palace
Sooner than expected, and then planned to
Get a head start for Arden in the morning.
When they were two miles outside the city
Of Gunter, they were overtaken by a rider,
Who carried a message from Prince Paragon.
On tearing open the letter, Frederic read,
"Come quickly, bring the fruit that heals
All wounds. While attending Independence
Day Parade, my father and I were attacked
By assassins. King Hooligan has suffered
Severe injury, although I remain unharmed."

After he had read Prince Paragon's letter,
Frederic became distraught, and instantly
Turned back, in the direction of the city.
Once they arrived at the palace, Frederic
Hurried inside to tell Prince Paragon bad
News, saying, "Alas, I have no more fruit.
The final one, my Physician used to treat
My wife, Kathleen, who nearly died from a
Mortal blow. What's left Edmund controls."
This shocked Prince Paragon, who believed
That Frederic had come to help his father,
Who lay on the bed, still and unconscious.

When Frederic saw how much Prince Paragon
Wanted to get his hands on the holy fruit,
He said, "Come join with me then, while I
Return to Arden and then once more resume
Command of my army; together, we can take
The Tree of Life and its fruit, that will
Heal your father, King Hooligan, who lies
Asleep in bed, made pitiful by his wounds."
Persuaded, Prince Paragon said, "So be it.
Since this fruit is my father's only hope
At life, I'll risk all to gain possession
Of it, even if that means war with Edmund."

When Frederic arrived at the mountain camp,
In Arden, he went into the prison house to
Meet Edmund's old officer, General Rudolph,
And as promised, they drank a toast hoping
For a quick end to the war. After a glass
Of wine their conversation became friendly.
"Will you be able to trust the Pazmanians?"
General Rudolph asked, when he heard their
Ranks had joined together to oppose Edmund.
"For the time being," Frederic said, being
Honest. "The Pazmanians do whatever serves
Their best interests. I have no illusions."

The Pazmanians are an odd, even mysterious
People," General Rudolph said. "They have
A society unlike any other nation on earth.
Their women remain indoors while their men
Go free in the open. They only teach boys
In the arts of war, at which they do excel."
Frederic agreed with General Rudolph, when
He said, "Yes, I saw no women while I rode
In Gunter, except a few dark eyes flirting
From windows, as I passed by on the street.
Their society is militaristic, with people
Under constant surveillance and harassment."

"Let me give you sound advice about Edmund,"
General Rudolph said. "Don't hesitate, or
Postpone your attack to negotiate with him.
Edmund can't be trusted to do what he says."
Frederic thought for a moment, then smiled.
"I believe I've learned my lesson, General."
It was then, as Frederic stood up to leave,
General Rudolph quickly stood at attention
And saluted by clicking his heels together
Like a Prussian officer. "I thank you for
Visiting me," General Rudolph said, bowing.
"I wish you good luck when fighting Edmund."

Edmund Devises A New Plan

Meanwhile, when back at Longhengren Castle,
Where Ambassador Bourbon had sought asylum,
Edmund listened quietly, as the Ambassador
Explained how all the assassins had failed
To murder Prince Paragon and King Hooligan,
When he said, "The unexpected had happened.
Who knew that Prince Paragon would move at
The last minute, saying that nature called
Him and he had to visit an outdoor latrine?
This left King Hooligan, alone and exposed,
But still surrounded by many palace guards,
Who my assassins went through to wound him."

Edmund felt disappointed by this news, but
He seemed more philosophical, when he said,
"Let's not cry over spilt milk as a maiden
Who ruins her day by tipping over the pail.
We must ensure the success of our new plan.
Repeat back to me what you are going to do."
The Ambassador thought for a moment before
He said, "When we reach the spot where the
Pazmanian army lies encamped on the border,
I will tell our commander, General Flavius,
That King Hooligan is wounded and that I'm
To take command of the full Pazmanian army."

"Excellent," Edmund said, in the hope that
This plan to deceive them proved effective.
"By working together, our two armies shall
Defeat everything Frederic can throw at us.
Let us drink vintage wine from our cellars
And then toast our greatest enterprise yet."
After a servant had brought them wine on a
Tray, the Ambassador said, "I feel this is
Only the beginning of a long and beautiful
Relationship." Then immediately, to bring
Good luck, they drank red wine and smashed
Two glasses, tossing them in the fireplace.

However, as it often happens in this world,
Few endeavors go exactly according to plan.
In a few days, when the Ambassador arrived
At camp and then told General Flavius that
He had orders, authorized by King Hooligan,
To take over command of the Pazmanian army,
General Flavius offered a strong objection,
Saying, "This may be true, Ambassador; but
I must stay in command, until I have heard
From Prince Paragon, who lives in spite of
An attack by assassins." This decision by
General Flavius suddenly cost him his life,

When he became encircled by several guards,
Who drew knives and then stabbed him. Now,
With Ambassador Bourbon in control, all of
The Pazmanian army crossed the unseen line
Between the two borders, and joined Edmund,
Whose army had surrounded the Tree of Life.
There they waited for a week, anticipating
The arrival of Frederic's army, which came
One week later, and instantly prepared for
Battle by the formation of three phalanxes.
But, seeing his army was of a smaller size,
Frederic delayed an attack for another day.

This was done so Prince Paragon would have
Time to sneak into the Pazmanian camp, and
Speak to his Generals who were still loyal,
When he boldly arrived to visit their tent,
One evening, and said, "All of my father's
Assassins were hired by Ambassador Bourbon.
Him you are to find, then summarily arrest."
However, Ambassador Bourbon succeeded once
Again in deceiving Prince Paragon, when he,
That master of disguises, was able to slip
Passed the guards, under cover of darkness,
By dressing up in the costume of a servant.

That very same evening, inside of his tent,
Frederic talked about strategy with Prince
Paragon, and together they made a decision.
They'd attack Edmund's army at first light.
But it too didn't happen according to plan.
The reason being, Edmund withdrew his army
During the night, although they could hear
Workers digging trenches, with shovels and
Pickaxes, and they could look up and see a
Thousand campfires glowing on the hillside.
This was part of Edmund's elaborate scheme
To make them think his army had bivouacked,

When in fact, the majority of Edmund's men
Had withdrawn, under the cover of darkness,
After having muted the noise of the wagons,
By wrapping all four wheels in cotton rags,
And by ordering all of the men to be quiet,
And follow the only man who held a lantern.
The plan worked so well, it totally fooled
Frederic and Prince Paragon, who came from
Their tents the next morning, expecting to
Join in battle, but instead were amazed to
See Edmund had slipped away unnoticed, and
Had left behind a rearguard to oppose them.

But, even this small rearguard had already
Begun marching toward the main army, which
Everyone, including the enlisted men, knew
Was in rapid retreat to Longhengren Castle,
The giant fortress, whose towers and walls
Had withstood a cycle of invaders for ages.
Suddenly, Frederic saw the column of smoke
Rising in the sky and knew that Edmund had
Set the Tree of Life afire rather than let
It fall in the hands of his despised enemy,
Whose wounds could be healed time and time
Again, if they used the power of its fruit.

Feeling a deep sense of despair over what
Happened, Frederic noticed two men riding
Toward him, carrying a large green banner,
Embroidered with an image showing a black
Dragon, the symbol of Pazmania, and so in
This way he had recognized Prince Paragon,
Who had seen the gray column of smoke too,
And had come at once out of growing alarm.
"Edmund goes to seek refuge in the castle.
But I'll make its walls unsafe," Frederic
Said. "First, we rescue the Tree of Life,
Whose fruit is far more desired than gold."

"Lead the way there," Prince Paragon said,
"My soldiers will soon follow this banner."
So Frederic raced his white horse Absalom
Into the lead, as Prince Paragon followed
Over the hill where they both stopped and
Stared, horrified at what they saw, below.
There was the Tree of Life, what was left
Of the trunk and branches, now reduced to
A bony skeleton, a pile of penitent ashes
And charcoal. Edmund had carried off all
Of its fruit, except for the pieces which
Lay smashed and burned, leaving them none.

Just then, they saw four monks with hoods
On their heads, circling the Tree of Life,
Their worshipful voices raised in singing
Songs, chants, prayers, even incantations,
To the Lord of all creation, who shall be
A living mystery, even to the end of time.
When Frederic realized the reason why the
Four monks were doing these ancient rites,
In the hope God would intercede on behalf
Of the Tree of Life, through divine mercy,
His chest heaved with sorrow, while large
Tears rolled down the sides of his cheeks.

O Father, Holy Ghost, and Son,
O Tree of Life what have they done?
Forgive sins seven times seven.
This you do to go to Heaven.
O Father, Holy Ghost, and Son,
O Tree of Life what damage done?
We ask you remove the evil
That was conjured by the Devil.

O Father, Holy Ghost, and Son,
O Tree of Life, be thou as one.
An exorcism is the thing
To now remove the painful sting
Of death, destruction, and decay,
Forever, starting with today.
Quick, up to Heaven you go,
Up, up, up, over the rainbow.

What battle has thou lost and won?
There is no death in the holy one.
No sorrows, no sighs, and no tears,
No horrors, no evils, and no fears.
Prepare you now for the journey
Which you buy for only a penny.
Go lickety, lickety, lickety split,
When we touch you, you are it.

Quick, kneel down on thy knee,
And pray the Lord is with thee.
Heaven won't wait another day.
So I say again, and again I say:
Now all three are in one.
O Father, Holy Ghost, and Son,
O Tree of Life, be fast and not slow,
Back to the dawn of ages, go.

Better is a Tree in Heaven's garden
Than to be a King in Hell's kitchen.

Then suddenly, soon as the chant had ended,
The Tree of Life began to vibrate and fade
Dimly, like it existed betwixt and between
Opposing realms, those of Heaven and Earth,
When presto, it vanished in puffs of smoke,
Leaving four monks lying prone in the dirt.
Now Frederic could hardly believe his eyes
When all of the monks stood up, and one of
Them quickly came up to him, with his feet
Invisible under the long brown robe, which
Made his body appear to float above ground.
With his hood removed, Frederic recognized

The headmaster from the old Abbey of Trent,
Monsignor Saint Pierre who had helped save
Him, much earlier, when he had almost died
From the black Dragon's bite. So Frederic
Said to him, "Why are you here? The field
Of battle is no place for gentle monks who
Live in quiet prayers, grace, and solitude."
"Since you ask I will tell you," Monsignor
Pierre said. "We came to the Tree or Life,
Hoping to take its fruit back to the Abbey,
For our brother who lies sick in bed. But,
As everyone can see, Edmund has burned the

Tree of Life, which we wanted to save, but
Could not, even if we had come from hiding,
Since Edmund wished the monks slain. Have
You some fruit to give us?" When Frederic
Answered, "I've none to give you. Neither
Have I any fruit for a dying King Hooligan,"
Monsignor Pierre revealed, without knowing
Who Prince Paragon was, "News of his death
And of the death of the black Dragon would
Be welcome, for we have suffered much from
Their evil deeds." Now, these words upset
Prince Paragon, who reached for his dagger.

Just then, Prince Paragon spit in the face
Of the old monk and then said, "Watch what
You say about my father, King Hooligan, or
I swear, I shall cut out your lying tongue,
You Christian dog!" Quickly, Frederic had
To hold Prince Paragon by his right arm to
Stop him from removing the dagger from his
Waistband; realizing his mistake, the monk
Said, "Please forgive me. I spoke harshly,
Without thinking. The passing away of the
Tree of Life sets all of our teeth on edge,
Since we die, without benefit of its fruit."

Now, in response to the old monk's remarks,
Prince Paragon reminded Frederic about the
Small black control box, still in Edmund's
Possession. "I shall pardon this old monk,
Who comes from a monastery, where solitude
And the study of books have made him crazy.
This control box belongs to all the people
Of Pazmania, who want to see the return of
A beloved and worshipped god, Aquilasaurus.
I'll hold you responsible if the black box
Vanishes," Prince Paragon said to Frederic,
Who had recognized it as the veiled threat

That it was and then nodded in recognition
Of the fact. Just then, several Pazmanian
Officers, on horseback, rode up wanting to
Talk with their Prince concerning an issue
Of great importance. Meanwhile, Monsignor
Pierre took Frederic aside, and then spoke
To him, saying, "I meant what I said about
King Hooligan, and the black Dragon, which
Must be killed, since it shall destroy all
That Ardenians hold sacred." But Frederic
Said nothing more, and rode Absalom toward
Longhengren Castle, in front of his armies.

Aquilasaurus Kills Prince Paragon

After about one month of continuous siege,
In which Frederic was able to cut off the
Water supply to the castle by diverting a
Stream, King Edmund realized the hour had
Come, when he freed the god, Aquilasaurus,
Which leaped from the iron barred cage on
The instant and then spread out its wings
And flew upward to perch on the belltower,
Where the green hills rolled on for miles.
From here the haughty black Dragon looked
Down below at an army ten thousand strong,
As the lord and master of all it surveyed.

As soon as Prince Paragon set his eyes on
The god, Aquilasaurus, he was obsessed by
The desire to capture that creature alive,
And throwing caution to the wind, he went
Out alone to conquer the black Dragon, in
The belief that it would obey his command.
Sensing the kill, the black Dragon leaped
From the belltower, with wings like a bat,
Upon which it could glide through the air,
Without effort, and then fell steadily to
Earth, stopping just a few feet away from
Prince Paragon, who stood beside the road.

Wanting to get in close, yet avoid danger,
Prince Paragon came up and tried to lasso
The god, Aquilasaurus, just when it moved
Its head and then dodged the big rope net.
Before Prince Paragon could throw the net
Again, the black Dragon instantly pounced
And then stung him unconscious, utilizing
The pointed barb on its long tapered tail.
Then everyone stared in silent horror, as
The black Dragon tore Prince Paragon into
Pieces, using beak and talons like a hawk,
When it plucks out the feathers of a dove.

Frederic Slays The Black Dragon

In the meantime, Frederic ran out to pick
Up the net, from where it lay in the dirt,
In the hopes of trapping the black Dragon,
Which continued to peck at Prince Paragon,
Who now lay dead, his flesh stripped from
His bones, exposing the fact that all men
Have white skulls. But, the black Dragon,
With surprisingly quick reflexes, reached
The place, first, and in one simultaneous
Movement, tossed the hoop through the air
And down over his head, pinning both arms,
So that Frederic couldn't reach the sword.

Now Frederic knew he was in for the fight
Of his life when he struggled for freedom
And then tripped over the net and fell on
His back in the dirt. Without skipping a
Beat, the black Dragon landed at his side,
So close, Frederic could smell the stench
Of its breath. Then, two things happened.
The black Dragon threw back its head, and
Cried loudly in defiance, while the metal
Blade on the Sword of Tarsus grew red hot
And burnt a hole in the net, large enough
So that Frederic could release both hands.

On the instant he pressed on the blinking
Blue sapphire embedded in the gilded hilt,
Activating the cloaking stealth mechanism,
Frederic became invisible and slipped out
From the net. Confused, the black Dragon
Immediately lashed out with its long tail,
Which Frederic soon ducked to avoid being
Clubbed in the head. Then Frederic stood
Up, raised his arms in the air, and swung
The Sword of Tarsus to severe the head of
God, Aquilasaurus, the great eagle lizard,
Ending its power to wage war with mankind.

This death of the black Dragon caused the
Ardenians to cheer at the moment Frederic
Became visible again, holding up the head
Like a trophy; but, the Pazmanians became
Silent, as soon as they saw what happened,
And then mourned for the black Dragon and
Prince Paragon. Days ago, they had heard
The news concerning King Hooligan's death
From severe wounds inflicted by assassins,
And now, they had lost their black Dragon,
The god, Aquilasaurus. They could choose
War; uncertain, Frederic prayed for peace.

At that very moment, to Frederic's relief,
It appeared the Pazmanians would withdraw,
Having lost their desire to battle Edmund.
Only a few soldiers left in the beginning,
Then gradually the whole army of Pazmania
Started marching in the direction of home.
As he stood there, with shiny metal armor,
Now smeared with the black Dragon's blood,
Frederic watched, in silence, as officers
Carried away the body of their Prince and
Asked him for the black Dragon's head too.
This Frederic refused, and said, "I claim

The prize I justly won by right of battle.
I shall show you what happens to traitors."
Suddenly, Frederic gave the order for his
Men to put the black Dragon's head within
A catapult, and sling it over the wall of
Longhengren Castle, much to the amazement
Of the Pazmanians, who also stayed behind
To watch, as they incinerated its carcass
To destroy the germs, and then learned it
Was neither meat, nor metal, but a hybrid
Made by Togalons, who were annihilated by
Their own weapons in a terrible civil war.

The defenders inside of Longhengren Castle
Had realized they were in dire straits, as
Teams of engineers worked around the clock
To divert the stream away from the cistern,
Denying any water source for the occupants,
Who would rather slowly die of thirst than
Surrender. In four weeks, when grain bins
Grew empty and hunger spread in the castle
Walls, the people who were healthy carried
The sick and dead from the houses and then
Laid them in the streets, where eventually
Packs of dogs came and ate their carcasses.

In addition, bombardments with stones from
The catapults continued, all day and night,
Along with oil pots that set houses ablaze
In the courtyard. But one man in all this
Realized that to continue the battle would
Be futile; right now compromise was needed.
This man was none other than the Pazmanian,
Ambassador Bourbon, who, as a plan of last
Resort, sent his old servant with a letter
Written to Frederic, in which he described
The situation there and asked for a pardon,
In exchange for pulling open the main gate.

Frederic approved the plan, which happened
On the first dark moonless night, when the
Shadows hid the actions of the old servant,
Who had raised the bars from the main gate,
Only to be caught two minutes later by the
Officer on duty, who realized too late, he
Could not stop enemy soldiers from pouring
In the main gate and consequently took the
Old servant upstairs, where Edmund now ate
Supper with his friend, Ambassador Bourbon,
Who looked up in horror at his old servant
And then dropped a spoon in his onion soup.

"Come on, you old gadfly, speak the truth!"
The guard said, shaking him by the collar.
"Tell King Edmund what happened, not more
Than five minutes ago!" When the old man
Failed to speak, and trembled like a leaf,
The guard slapped his face, and then said
To King Edmund, "I caught this rat in the
Act of letting the enemy in the main gate.
He told me his master, Ambassador Bourbon,
Had put him up to a crime of treason most
Foul; he told me the Ambassador had hoped
For an amnesty. What shall I do with him?"

When the old servant looked at his master,
Ambassador Bourbon, just then, he pleaded,
"I beg your forgiveness; but I must think
Of my wife and two small children at home."
"Shut up, you miserable fool!" Ambassador
Bourbon shouted, "You will murder us both!"
Suddenly, Ambassador Bourbon swung around
To stare at King Edmund, and said, "I can
Easily explain what happened, King Edmund."
But just then, they heard soldiers coming
Upstairs, each one swearing an oath, they
Would murder King Edmund. At that moment,

Ambassador Bourbon leaped up from a table
And then ran toward the doorway, thinking
If he could reach the courtyard, he could
Give himself up to a squadron of soldiers.
However, just at that moment, King Edmund
Sprang from the table, as nimble as a cat.
He took the officer's long spear and then
Threw it, hard as he could, at Ambassador
Bourbon, sticking the point of that blade
In the middle of his back, causing him to
Scream, as he suddenly fell down, impaled,
When about five feet short of the doorway.

King Edmund felt vindicated, because long
Practice at martial arts had succeeded in
Destroying his enemy; turning to face the
Officer, he said, "Go help our troops who
Contend for the castle, while I search in
My drawer and burn up sensitive documents."
The officer looked askance at the servant,
And then asked, "What shall I do with him?"
Now King Edmund stared at the old servant,
Whom he hated for his betrayal, then said,
"Kill him!" So, the guard quickly obeyed,
And ran that old man through with a sword.

Right after that on duty officer had gone,
King Edmund stared at the Ambassador, who
Lay face down on his stomach, alive still,
Although pinned to the floor with a spear.
While Ambassador Bourbon grimaced in pain,
Saying nothing at all, King Edmund mocked
Him, saying, "Where are all of your sweet
Honeyed words, your refined speeches that
Kept my advisers guessing your intentions?
Where is your art, your eloquent rhetoric
That reveals subtle truths, your whispers
Which poured poisons in the people's ears?

Why glum and silent now? It's like a cat,
In the old adage, who looked for a rat in
The alley and by accident was caught in a
Trap; even the alley cat knew how to howl."
Just then, King Edmund opened the drawers
In his desk and spilled their contents on
The floor, which he then lit with a flame
From the candle. It was only then, after
He had left that room in a ball of flames,
He heard Ambassador Bourbon screaming for
Help. But, showing no mercy, King Edmund
Headed for the sanctuary of the belltower.

King Edmund Bargains With Satan

King Edmund had passed a long dreary night,
Alone in the belltower, where he felt cold,
Hungry, and miserable due to loss of sleep.
Early in the morning, at the crack of dawn,
With his spirit weighed down by depression,
He considered the possibility of surrender,
When talking to no one but himself, saying,
"Dream derives from dream, since the world
Is an illusion, and all my proud endeavors
Have come to nothing, and soon end in this
Sad state of affairs here in the belltower.
A King may hang his dreams among the stars.

But, even the great plans are knocked down
Like a tower made of children's woodblocks.
I wanted to be well thought of, but people
Despise me; I wanted to be loved, but they
Only curse behind my back, and say hateful
Things, hoping that I will fall from grace.
But, I have grown weary and no longer care
How anyone regards me; if the world should
End tomorrow, it would not be quick enough.
I'm past caring, past loving, past feeling,
After I bargained with the Devil, and lost."
At that moment King Edmund put on his cape,

And then stepped back in horror, as he saw
A live image of Satan appear in the lining.
"What is the meaning of this feckless talk?"
Satan said, anger turned his face dark red.
"Your mission lies mostly undone; Frederic
Breathes and walks the Earth like an Angel.
Have you forgotten your promise to destroy
His many Christ like qualities?" Suddenly,
King Edmund went crazy. "I'll crucify him!"
He said. "Do it very soon," Satan replied,
Before he disappeared, "Frederic comes now.
Here is your chance to fulfill the promise."

Meanwhile, the rebellion had been put down
And all the rebels imprisoned, all but one
That is, King Edmund, who had continued to
Elude detection. When it became day again,
Chester Dune, who had won honor during the
Battle, came up to Frederic, and then said,
With a deep solemnity that deserved notice,
"We have found two bodies, so badly burned
It is impossible to recognize any features.
I fear that King Edmund may be one of them."
To which Frederic said, "Show me where you
Have laid them, after you put out the fire.

I would recognize my brother, Edmund, even
If his ashes were poured into a marble urn."
"Surely you jest, sire," Chester Dune said.
"Perhaps I do a little," Frederic said, as
He followed Chester Dune into that chamber,
Now a hollowed out ruin with burnt timbers.
"I fear that neither of these poor rascals
Are Edmund, who must still be within these
Castle walls," Frederic said, as he looked
At both corpses, burned beyond recognition.
"If I knew Edmund's hiding place, I'd soon
Give him the justice he so justly deserves."

Now, as Frederic went to the window to get
A breath of fresh air, he happened to look
Toward the belltower, and then noticed the
Flock of pigeons that were circling around
The tall pointed spire, and recognized the
Fact something had disturbed those pigeons.
It was right then that Frederic remembered
His childhood when Edmund liked to hide in
The belltower, whenever they played a game
Of Hide and Seek. Edmund must be up there,
Frederic thought, just then, as he spun on
His heels and ran for the belltower, alone.

Frederic Kills The Baby Dragon

Frederic went on by the equestrian stables,
Without bothering to stop there, and dress
In his white armor, which hung on the wall,
Waiting for his squire to scrub and polish,
After washing off the black Dragon's blood.
He might need it never entered in his mind,
Because Frederic felt confident having the
Sword of Tarsus by him, now buckled around
His waist. Soon, he climbed up the flight
Of stairs that would lead to the belltower,
Taking two steps at once, until he reached
There, and then paused to catch his breath.

Now hoping to see Edmund's image reflected
In the small rectangle, on the upper blade
Of the sword, Frederic became disappointed
When he saw none. Frederic was unaware of
The fact that the Sword of Tarsus had lost
Some of its powers, because it had gone by
A service schedule for routine maintenance.
Nevertheless, as he turned the last corner
On the stairs, Frederic heard that buzzing
Noise, which indicated something small had
Set off the warning alarm, and in two more
Steps, there it was, the baby Black Dragon,

Which violently hissed from where it stood
At the top, its back hunched up like a cat.
Acting fast, before it had time to leap in
The air, Frederic noticed a blinking light,
Then pressed on the emerald with his thumb.
Instantly, a ribbon of flame shot out from
The Sword of Tarsus, and then engulfed the
Baby black Dragon, causing it to shriek in
Pain, one second before it was incinerated
And turned into a grease spot on the floor.
Frederic felt relieved, since the creature
Had missed poking out his eyes with talons.

However, Frederic wasn't out of danger yet.
King Edmund lurked inside of the belltower,
Where he had used the baby black Dragon as
A military tactic known in the parlance as
A diversion, as a way to distract Frederic
For the fraction of a second needed by him
To reach out with his arms and then plunge
The sword deep into Frederic's tender neck,
Splitting him almost in half with a single
Powerful stroke, learnt from many years of
Constant practice at fighting mock battles.
Instantly, Frederic fell backward down the

Stairs, coming to rest on the biggest step,
With the blade of Edmund's sword lodged in
His flesh. Edmund had dealt a severe blow
And had knocked the Sword of Tarsus out of
Frederic's hands so that it lay at the top
Of the stairs, which Edmund had to pass by
On his way down the stairs to see Frederic,
Over whom he straddled with both legs, and
Began to gloat, relish his triumph, saying,
"My brother is dead. Now I will be called
Edmund, the King of Arden, thanks to Satan,
My talisman, and cleverness, my only guide."

But this victory was brief, because Edmund
Was unfamiliar with the mysterious ways of
The Sword of Tarsus, which quickly started
To roll sideways, on its multifaceted ruby,
Until the blade stopped opposite of Edmund,
Who heard unusual noises of unknown origin,
And then turned around, just as the tip of
The blade suddenly flew off from the Sword
Of Tarsus and then struck him in the chest.
Realizing that he was falling, Edmund held
The rope, unsteadily, while the bells rang
Out from the tower, dong, dang, dong, dang.

Even in this dire situation, the irony was
Not missed by King Edmund, who soon became
Too weak to hold on and slid down the rope,
Until he nearly fell on top of his brother,
Frederic, mired in a mingled pool of blood,
And listened to the bell's last dying peal.
As King Edmund lay there, he heard pigeons
In the loft, and then heard someone coming
Up the steps, near the bottom of the tower,
And for a moment King Edmund believed that
His wound was slight and he might be saved.
This happened just before he saw the Devil.

Immediately, King Edmund became afraid and
Then said, in a trembling voice, "Why have
You returned so soon after I have murdered
My brother, Frederic?" Satan then drew so
Near that Edmund could see his yellow eyes,
Dark and sinister, the embodiment of death.
His face was red, the color of dried blood,
And on his head were two horns like a goat.
"The hour has come. Now you must pay your
Debt," Satan said. But King Edmund didn't
Want to leave, and he said, "Frederic lies
In the sleep that mimics death, and proves

That I have kept my promise; what more can
I do?" Satan answered, "Come here, Edmund!
You cannot live a minute longer. You have
Burnt down the Tree of Life; your sentence
Is death." King Edmund struggled as Satan
Pulled on his legs, with long creepy hands,
And then quickly tore his spirit right out
Of his body, like a white handkerchief out
Of a coat pocket. Terribly afraid of what
He will find in Hell, King Edmund screamed.
Then, almost immediately, Monsignor Pierre
Appeared at the top steps of the belltower.

The Brave Knight's Solemn Epilogue

A little before this, Monsignor Pierre had
Fingered prayer beads, as he knelt down at
The altar, right below the belltower, when
He had heard the bells ringing and decided
To determine its cause, by making the long
Climb, all the way up the flight of stairs.
On turning around the corner, the evidence
Of what happened here quickly became clear.
Then after five minutes more, everyone who
Had heard the bells dropped what they were
Doing, then climbed the belltower steps to
Join the old monk, who stood there already.

One of those among the assembled crowd was
The brave Knight, Chester Dune, who turned
His eyes away from the terrible scene, and
Then wept, before saying to everyone there,
"Let us teach in school, by a proclamation
Of the senate, lessons we learn here today.
Let us lay these two brothers next to King
Harold, within the same white marbled tomb,
So they may find peace in death, what they
Could not do in life, being contrary souls.
I shall not call our King Edmund a traitor,
Though he took the crown from Frederic who

Promised good things, yet miserably failed,
Which all too often is the fate of mankind.
If we are to learn from this great tragedy,
Let us remember our nation is a cluster of
Many families, and therefore shall reflect
What those families do, either good or bad.
Please join me, then, as we carry each one
In solemn procession to the memorial place,
Where years from now, their story shall be
Told to a new generation, which must learn
Again the golden rule that teaches good is
Better than evil, always and forever, Amen."

Just then, everyone learned from Monsignor
Pierre that someone ran from the belltower,
Just seconds before he got there, and that
He had with him the broken Sword of Tarsus.
"Just imagine the mischief that may happen,
If the weapon has fallen in the hands of a
Thief, who has unscrupulous principles and
Who may become like King Edmund in that he
Could make the world suffer all over again,
By making all those in it bend to his will,
And accept his authority, on pain of death,"
Monsignor Pierre said, acting very shocked.

For none knew better than Monsignor Pierre
The old saying, history repeats itself and
Total power corrupts totally. He believed
They were factually correct and that these
Circumstances must be avoided at all costs.
The very reason why he had thought it best
To quickly hide the broken Sword of Tarsus
In the inner folds of his long Monk's robe,
Before others had time to reach that scene.
Even for years afterward, Monsignor Pierre
Worried that one day someone will discover
His secret, and so the Priest said nothing.

This small secret would be between him and
The Lord, since no one else must ever know
What happened that day, when he arrived at
The Abbey of Trent, and then took the long
Hike to the side of the mountain, and then
Hid that sword, in the same mound where he
Had buried Tarsus, who had owned the sword,
And the ruby, from which it extruded power.
In addition, Monsignor Pierre also removed
The ruby as a precaution so that the sword
May never be used again as a tool of death.
Where the ruby is no one knows to this day.

THE END

ACKNOWLEDGMENTS

It would be impossible to list all of the influences that have gone into the making of this book. However, I would like to mention that I have been fascinated by Near Death Experiences for many years, and that I have drawn inspiration from many sources, some of which have ended up in this epic poem, FREDERIC, THE KING OF ARDEN.

Although Near Death Experiences have always been around, there is one major difference, between those of today and those of yesterday. In the middle ages, in Europe, a person who confessed to having one of these experiences would mostly likely be accused of being a sorcerer, witch, blasphemer, or heretic. Also, they might be severely punished for their transgression, even unto death. At the very least, they would be thought of as being crazy. This should not surprise anyone, since even Jesus Christ himself was accused of being Beelzebub, who was a kind of demon from Hell. Thank God this prejudice is disappearing from the world.

Finally, I would encourage anyone with an interest in Near Death Experiences to seek out the testimonies of those people who have had them. One good source, where you can see videos of people giving their testimonies, is on Youtube.com. In addition to this, there are many good books written on the subject, which can be found in stores and on Internet websites. I strongly suggest that you read them. They just may make a believer out of you, and then change your life, forever. I know they have changed mine.

Kent Dellaire

www.ingramcontent.com/pod-product-compliance
Lightning Source LLC
Chambersburg PA
CBHW071228260626
47162CB00004B/1473